THE DUCK POND

And Ten Other Short Stories.

Tim Morgetroyd.

Tim Morgetroyd Publishing

CHAPTER 1

The Duck Pond.

"Daddy, am I a good girl?"

"You have always been a good girl," said the man sitting on the park bench as he held his small daughter tightly in his arms and looked at the duck pond that only had one duck. The duck was at the far end of the pond and had stopped swimming.

"If I'm a good girl, why am I sick?" asked the child in a weak voice that made her Father close his eyes and try not to cry. The Father was trying to think of an answer that would make sense to a little girl only 7 years old dying of cancer who had only days or maybe hours to live, but all he could think was how unfair it was. He had told the doctors and nurses it wasn't fair, and anybody who asked him how sick she was, but he couldn't make himself tell his daughter she was dying because life isn't always fair.

"I don't know why your sick, sweetheart," he heard himself say. He held her a little tighter and knew he couldn't let her die thinking she was sick because she was being punished. He tried to think like a child and asked himself if he was his daughter's age and worried he had cancer because he was bad, what could his Mother or Father have said to him? Then the words came to him and he opened his eyes and looked down at his daughter's pale face and looked deep into her large sad blue eyes.

"If people got sick because they were bad, all the bad people would be in hospitals. But I know a lot of bad people who never get sick," he said slowly, "Some of them grow very old, and they never have to go to a hospital."

"Not ever?" asked his daughter.

"Not ever."

"But lots of good people get sick, so they didn't get sick because they are bad."

He kissed the top of his daughter's head, and said softly, "When you were in the hospital, you had wonderful friends and 3 of them died. They weren't bad people, were they?"

The child shook her head, and said "I miss them so much." She rested her head against his chest, and her small body felt so light from all the weight she had lost.

"Wasn't it nice of the Doctor's to let me bring you here? I told them it was your favorite place, and soon all the Ducks would be gone for the Winter," he said, and he could feel the tears start rolling down his cheeks.

The child was very quiet for a long time, then said in an almost whisper, "I like the Ducks."

"Why do you think that Duck is still here? I think that Duck stayed behind because he was waiting for you to come visit," he whispered like it was a big secret only the two of them should know.

"Daddy."

"What sweetheart?"

"When I get to Heaven, will my hair grow back?"

"Oh yes," said the Father, surprised at how much he believed it when he wasn't sure if there was a Heaven. He kissed the top of her hat so she could feel the kiss on her bald head, and know if Daddy kissed her head he could make it all better.

"I'm sorry Daddy and the Doctors couldn't make you better. I know I promised you we would make you better. We tried very hard. Just like we tried to make your mommy better. I thought she was just tired, but in a few months she was gone."

"I miss Mama."

"So do I," he said. He lowered his voice like he was confiding a secret, and whispered, "Sometime your mommy and I would argue and mommy would cry, but we always loved each other. And your mommy didn't get sick and die because she was a bad person, did she?"

He felt his daughter's head on his chest silently answer him as she shook her head "No." Then he heard her weak voice say like she was sharing a big secret, "Mama was in my dream last night." She paused, then spoke slowly and with a diamond hard faith only a child has, "She told me I was going to see her again."

The father started crying. He heard his daughter trying to say something, and finally she whispered a few words he could barely hear. As he moved his ear close to her mouth her heard her say,"You're my hero." He felt the warm tears rolling down his cheeks, and a sudden pain in his chest made him squeeze his eyes shut and grit his teeth. His chest pains had started a week ago and he hadn't told the Doctors or Nurses. He pressed his left hand against his chest and took slow breaths, then opened his eyes and stared at the Duck at the far end of the pond and the Duck was so still and the pond's water so still it was like looking at the most beautiful painting he had ever seen.

He was suddenly very tired, and was trying to keep his eyes open, and he heard a voice that sounded like his voice say, "I know a man who is so bad he lost all his friends, and his wife left him and moved far away, and she won't come home to see their little girl who is very sick."

"Why is he bad?" asked the child.

"He had a big company that made a lot of money, and his company had to get rid of dangerous chemicals. And to save money, he had those chemicals buried nearby, right next to a schoolyard. And children playing in that schoolyard got sick, and some died. He was a bad man, but he had a little daughter who loved him. She was the only good thing that ever happened to him. Then one day she got very sick, and he doesn't want to live without her."

"What happened to him?"

"I don't know."

He sighed, then felt a sharp pain in his chest. He bent his head down and his right hand was under his daughter's chin and his hand gently lifted her face so he could look at her face and look into her eyes. Her eyes were closed, and as her lips moved he couldn't hear what she was saying. Her voice was so weak he had to put his ear close to her mouth, and he heard her whispering, "I don't want you to be alone." She fell asleep, and he could feel every one of the weak breaths she took pounding his chest like a fist.

He closed his tired eyes just to rest his eyes for a little while, but suddenly his eyes snapped open and he realized his arms were empty and his daughter was gone. He was full of panic as his eyes looked at the ground then left then right, and suddenly he saw the back of the pink coat and pink hat and his child was standing at the edge of the Duck Pond nearest to his bench. Before he could stand up and run to her to stop her falling in the water she suddenly turned to face him, and his body froze.

A miracle had happened.

She looked just like she did before she got sick. Her face was pink and rounder and her big blue eyes sparkled and her long chestnut hair had grown back, and she had gained back the weight she had lost and was bursting with energy. Her beautiful face was smiling at him, waiting for him to say something, then she turned and watched the only Duck in the pond swimming towards her. The Duck was half-way across the pond, and his daughter started running towards the duck, then suddenly she stopped right at the water's edge, turned around, and smiled the most beautiful smile he had ever seen. Her beautiful blue eyes were laughing and inviting him to come and chase the Duck with her. Then she turned and started running into the pond but her feet didn't touch the water. She was running on top of the water towards the Duck.

His eyes snapped open and his chin was resting on his chest and he lifted his head and felt the weight of her body in his arms. His right hand reached for her small right hand. Her hand was soft and cold and lifeless, and his left hand took off her pink hat and placed it on the bench as he kissed the top of her bald head. He looked out at the pond and saw the Duck was gone.

As his right hand held her hand his left hand reached inside his coat and felt the coat pocket. His hand pulled a paper out of the pocket, and with his left hand he opened the letter and held it. He had read it many times, but had to read it again:

"Dear Sir,

I am one of the parents whose children died after you and your company buried chemicals next to their schoolyard. My daughter was 8 when she got cancer. Her name was Sarah. She liked to play the piano, liked strawberry ice cream, and she loved animals. Sarah wanted to be a veterinarian.

She was a fighter, and fought her cancer for 2 years, 4 months, and 14 days. I never saw her cry until her hair fell out. Three days before her 11th Birthday she died in my arms in a hospital bed surrounded by her Father and 3 Sisters. She was crying because she wanted to say goodbye to her dog and the Hospital wouldn't allow her dog in the building.

My favorite picture of Sarah is in a frame on my living room wall, and it shows Sarah standing next to our piano that she loved to play. After she died, next to that picture I hung a similar picture of our piano, but where Sarah should be standing there is empty space. I miss her every day.

People at my church have told me I should try and forgive you. I can't speak for the other families, but I can't forgive you and I never will. One of my friends believes in Karma and believes you will pay a terrible price for what you did. I hope she is wrong, and you never have to watch helplessly as someone you love suffers and dies."

The Father finished reading the letter and stared at it. A sudden terrible pain in his chest made his hand drop the letter and grip his chest right below his heart. He was gasping for breath, and as the pain faded and he could breath again he leaned back against the bench. Hugging his daughter with both arms he stared across the empty pond at the dying sun's last rays of light, and a feeling of peace filled him as he waited.

The End

CHAPTER 2

Buffalo Tongues.

The sun was setting and the long dirt country road and trees and farmland would soon be hidden by the kind of total darkness you only see in the country at night when there is no moon or stars.

"I told you I would get us home before dark," said the man gripping the steering wheel of the car. He was grinning as he glanced at his wife in the passenger seat, but his wife ignored him and her eyes were staring through the windshield looking for their house.

"What's wrong?" he asked, his smile gone.

"I told you, I don't like strangers renting our house."

"You also said we can use the money."

"We *can* use the money," said his wife firmly.

"I'll never get used to how dark the nights are out here."

He heard his wife say "Maybe it's time we sold the place." She sounded like she was alone in the car and thinking out loud.

"We couldn't wait to move out of the city," he said, remembering how excited they had been to leave the city. He glanced at her face to see if she was serious. Maybe she's just tired, he thought. In the morning she might feel differently. But the idea sounded good. He looked straight ahead into the darkness and said "Why don't we talk about it tomorrow."

The road had been straight for miles and on both sides of the road there was only farmland and a few trees but up ahead on the right was a cluster of trees and as the car passed the trees the road curved right and there past the trees was their house. Behind their house the empty farmland stretched to the horizon where the sun had just vanished and the sun's dying glow burned red.

"Why are the lights on?" asked his wife.

"Maybe they left them on for us?" he suggested.

"If they left at 2 PM, the lights have been on since they left," said Joanna.

As the car passed the front of the house and turned right into the long driveway they saw a small white car parked by the side of their house. The husband slowed the car and parked behind the white car. "We can't kick them out, not at this hour," said the husband, waiting for his wife to convince him he was wrong. His wife was silent and he was glad the inside of the car was too dark to see her angry face.

"I guess this is the last time we rent to strangers," he said as he turned off the car's headlights and twisted the car keys dangling next to the steering wheel. The couple sat in the dark car, staring silently at the curtains of the front window that were lit from behind.

"They might be asleep," he said.

"Or in our bedroom and not sleeping," said the wife.

The husband opened his car door and got out, his eyes never leaving the front window as he slammed the car door shut. He heard his wife open the passenger door and close it, and they both walked to the front door. The husband was holding his car keys in his right hand and fumbled with the keys trying to find the key to the front door. The keys slid into the lock, and when he turned the key and pushed open the door he heard the sounds from the living room. A movie was playing on TV and a man and woman were laughing.

The husband walked in first, ready to shield his wife who was a few staps behind him. They both stopped and stared at the back of the two heads of the strangers sitting close together on the couch. The woman had very short black hair and the man had short blond hair. They were facing the large TV screen and on the screen was an old black and white movie showing Flying Saucers attacking a city. The special effects were so bad it was obvious the Flying Saucers were toys and the city was made of cardboard.

The man on the couch lifted an arm and pointed at the screen, and the two strangers laughed louder. Suddenly the woman's head turned around and looked at them. She jumped up and turned to face them. Her beautiful face was smiling. The man with her turned to see why she had jumped up and he smiled at them but remained sitting on the couch.

"You must be the owners," said the smiling brunette. She was strikingly beautiful and probably in her early 20's but looked younger, with big sparkling blue eyes in a very cute face, her short black hair cut in a cute haircut popular in the 1950's. She could have been plucked out of a 1950's Hollywood film, looking like one of those young innocent bubbly Hollywood starlets with cute faces and short dark hair and Las Vegas showgirl bodies. She and her boyfriend both could have stepped out of the silly 1950's B-Movie about Flying Saucers on the TV screen.

As she took a few steps towards him, Mark was trying not to stare at her large breasts and beautiful soft body that was squeezed into the tight short low-cut blue denim dress with shoulder straps over her bare shoulders. Her short dress showed off the most beautiful legs he had ever seen.

"Oh no!" said the smiling brunette, giggling as she said sweetly, "Nobody told you we were still here! Our car wouldn't start this afternoon, and we couldn't find anybody who would drive out here to fix it."

The man on the coach was young and handsome, in his

mid-20s, and as he stood up he looked like a poster for an American college football player. Standing next to his cute petite girlfriend they looked like a poster for the perfect young American couple. He looked embarrassed as he explained, "The house rental agency should have phoned you. We asked them to ask you if we could stay until you returned, and they didn't call us back so we assumed it was OK." The Brunette's cute face was begging them not to be angry.

The house's owners looked at each other and silently agreed this could have happened to anybody and they should be warm hosts to the stranded couple.

He and his wife relaxed, and as he said "I'm Mark and this is my wife Joanna," his wife pressed against him and her hand squeezed his arm. Mark looked at Joanna and saw her pretty face had a sweet half-smile and her eyes welcomed the strangers as if they were old friends. Mark was trying not to stare at the brunette as he said, "The Rental Company gave us your last names but didn't tell us your first names."

The man with blond hair moved closer to the short brunette as he said, "I'm Mike and this is my girlfriend Julie."

Mark said to the couple, "You can stay in our guest bedroom tonight, and we'll get a mechanic out here tomorrow."

"Are you sure?" smiled Julie, showing her beautiful white teeth as she bounced with excitement and looked up at her boyfriend.

"Of course," said Joanna. "It could have happened to anybody."

"Have you had dinner yet?" asked Mark.

Julie made a sad face and pouted playfully as she shook her head "No", and her boyfriend shook his head.

"How hungry are you?" smiled Mark.

"We're starving!" said Juie and Mike with one voice, and Julie giggled and pressed her body against Mike. Mike said to Mark, "The Rental Agency told us you were a well-known food critic, and we were looking at the books on your bookshelf about exotic food."

"Two of those books have my reviews on the back covers of the books."

"We read them!" said Mike excitedly.

"I have one of my favorite dishes in the fridge," said Mark. "Have you ever eaten Buffalo tongue?"

The two guests shook their heads "No."

Mark said, "Joanna doesn't like it, but you might."

The two guests looked at each other with happy faces and smiled.

Behind the living room was an open dining room and kitchen, and the dining table was long and made of dark wood and surrounded with 12 dark wood chairs. Behind the dining area the kitchen was so large and modern it could have been the set of a TV cooking show. Mark led the other three to the dining table, and pulled out a chair at the center of the table for his wife who always loved when he did that. He and his wife would be sitting facing the living room and front door, and the two guests would be together on the other side of the table facing their hosts.

Mark walked into the kitchen and got the plates and silverware, brought it out to the table and placed everything in front of his wife and guests and his own spot, then walked back to the kitchen and opened the massive doube-doored silver fridge. A small plate had a salad already prepared for his wife, and a plastic sealed container had six Buffalo tongues. He balanced the plate of salad on top of the plastic container and grabbed a full bottle of wine from the counter, and walked proudly back to the dining table. He saw Julie was facing his empty chair and Mike was facing his wife.

He put the dish with salad in front of his wife, and the bottle of wine and plastic container in the middle of the table. Behind him was a big mahognany cabinet with glass doors full of fancy dishes and cups and glasses, and he opened a door and took out four wine glasses and placed them on the table. He opened the wine bottle and poured wine into his wife's glass, then Julie's, then Mike's, then his his own glass.

He sat down and said "Anybody want to pray before we eat?" His wife laughed softly, Julie giggled, and Mike laughed loudest.

"Are you sure you want to try this?" he asked his guests.

Julie's cute innocent face smiled at him seductively,

and lust flashed in her eyes as she said playfully, "I'll try anything once." The top of her breasts and bare shoulders looked so white and soft and perfectly sculpted, and she leaned forward to look down at the plastic containter, letting him see down the top of her cleavage. Mark quickly lloked down at the plastic container and forced himself not to look at her. She's the most attractive woman I've ever seen, he thought, but after tomorrow I'll never see her again.

Mark opened the plastic container, stuck a fork in the meat, and placed a Buffalo tongue on Julie's plate, then his fork stabbed another tongue for Mike's plate, and the third tonge his for stabbed he put on his own plate. He looked at his wife who was enjoying eating her salad, and she seemed oblivious to Julie's flirting with him.

Mark took a bite of the meat, eating it slowly and loving its taste. He looked at Julie and Mike and saw them chewing, but their faces were blank. He smiled at his two guests and asked "What do you think?"

Julie's face brightened and she said excitedly "I like it!"

Mark looked at Julie's cleavage then at Mike. Mike's eyes were closed and he was chewing slowly. He stopped chewing and said, "I think I'm in love."

"You really love it?" asked Mark.

"We had a very long trip getting here, but it was worth it just to taste this," said Mike.

"Your serious, aren't you," said a delighted Mark.

"Very," said Mike.

Mark ate his Buffalo tounge slowly, savouring every bite just like the wine he was sipping in his glass, but he saw his guests eat their Buffalo tongues fast, and they were finished before he had eaten half his own tongue.

Mark put down his fork, lifted his wineglass and sipped the wine, and decided to say something about the History of the Buffalos. "When the first American cowboys came to the American West, they saw herds of Buffalos covering the valleys and hills as far as the eye could see. A few decades later Buffaloes were almost extinct, because the cowbys would kill a Buffalo just to eat its tongue. An Indian would kill a Buffalo and eat all the meat, use its all its fur, and even carve the bones, but the white men took the tongue and left the rest to rot."

"Aren't we doing the same thing right now?" asked Mike.

Mark looked at the meat on his plate, and said slowly, "If the Butcher threw out the meat and just sold the tongue, so what? I'm not eating hundreds of Buffalo Burgers so I can jusify eating one tongue." Mark picked up his fork and stabed a piece of the meat on his plate, and as he was about to take his next bite he stopped, thought a moment, and said, "Besides, if this Buffalo hadn't been killed, what would it be doing now? Discovering a cure for cancer?"

Mike burst out laughing and was looking at his girlfriend. His girlfriend had a naughty little smile and was staring down at her empty plate. Her smiling eyes lifted from her plate and looked deep into Mark's eyes. Mark swallowed the meat and lifted the wine bottle and filled his wife's empty wineglass, then lifted his own wineglass and said "A Toast. To the Buffalo who made this dinner possible."

Joanna lifted her wineglass and touched the glass to her husbands glass as the two guests sat stiffly, looking a little confused as they slowly lifted their wineglasses and a little awkwardly copied what Joanna was doing, clinking their glasses against their two hosts' wineglasses. The two guests suddenly smiled at each other then at their wineglasses like they had just learned a marvelous new trick.

Joanna eyed her two guests and asked, "Haven't you ever drunk a Toast before?"

"We don't drink much alcohol," said Mike.

"Do you do much travelling?" asked Joanna, sipping her wine and looking at the wine bottle to decide how much more she should drink.

"A LOT of travelling," giggled Julie, picking up her glass of wine and sipping it as her eyes glanced at her boyfriend to see his reaction.

Mike said, "Julie and I want to take a break from travelling. We were talking about buying a house in the country just like this one." He looked at his hosts and asked, "Have you ever thought about selling this place?"

Mark looked at his wife and saw his wife was looking at Mike like he had read her mind. He studied his wife's face a few seconds, and said "Funny you should ask that, but we were just talking about it."

Mike's serious face instanly beamed with a smile.

Julie's beautiful blue eyes were full of mischief as she stared deeply into Mark's eyes and purred "The bed in your bedroom looks soooo soft."

Mike sighed, and confessed, "I like a hard bed, but Julie's the boss in the bedroom."

"It's the softest bed I've ever slept in," said Joanna as she glanced at Julie, then her eyes fixed on Mike's face. Mike dabbed at his mouth with a napkin, then said "I'd love a tour of your property."

"Right now?" asked Mark.

Mike shrugged, then smiled. "If you show me around the property now, I can make you an offer then you and Joanna can sleep on it."

Mark looked at his wife, and she was staring at him full of excitement like it was the night before Christmas. She nodded at him and said, "We could sleep on it, and decide tomorrow before Mike and Julie leave." He felt his wife's hand on his leg, and her hand squeezed softly.

"It's really dark out, but it isn't cold," said Mark. He looked at Julie, who was bursting with excitement and smiling and her hands were under her chin silently clapping like a playful child.

"I've got a small flashlight in my car said Mike.

"I'm glad something in our car still works," giggled

Julie, giving her boyfriend a stern look.

Joanna laughed at Julie's joke, and emptied her wine glass.

Mike said to his hosts, "Thank you for the unforgettable dinner." He stood up and said to Mark, "I'll meet you outside," as he walked towards the front door.

Mike was already out the front door as Mark stood up and looked down at his wife's delighted face. Her eyes were promising him a night he'd never forget as soon as they were alone in their bedroom. Mike walked around the dining table towards the front door, glancing back at Joanna who was looking down at her empty plate and smiling.

Mike stepped through the front door into the warm black air, and couldn't see or hear Mike in the darkness. A sudden burst of light cutting a long bright slash in the darkness came from the flashlight in Mike's hand. Mark walked beside Mike towards the back of the house, the flashlight's spotlight giving colour to anything it touched.

"It's five acres," said Mark. "So you'll be cutting a lot of grass."

"I like the trees," said Mike, shining his light towards some trees.

"When Joanne and I first saw the place, I thought we could build a Treehouse if we had children."

Mike stopped walking, shone the flashlight in every direction, and stared silently at his host.

Mark felt himself becomining a little nervous as he looked at his guest's face, and forced a smile as he said, "Well, make me an offer."

Mike looked down at his feet, and said sadly, "Mark, I really like you."

Mark stiffened, and fear filled his body. How could he believe this stranger wanted to see his property at night? He forced himself to smile, and in his friendliest voice askd, "What are you trying to say, Mike." Maybey he could reason with Mike, talk him out of doing whatever terrible thing he was planning.

Mike's face was expressionless and his voice flat. He spoke slowly, in a low voice, "Mike isn't my real name, and my partner's name isn't Julie. There's nothing wrong with our car, and we don't want to buy your house." He stopped and was thinking hard about what to say next. "It's true we travelled a long way, and you wouldn't believe how far."

"How far?" asked Mark, certain he had to keep the stranger talking if he wanted to save his life and his wifes. If he didn't feel threatened he might just leave, and if he had escaped from a prison or mental hospital people were searching for him now, and they could be here soon.

"We came from out there," said the stranger, looking up to his right and glancing at the stars.

Mark heard himself blurt out "Where's the Flying Saucer."

"Like the ones in that movie?" asked the stranger. "If you saw what we use, you'd be disappointed. It looks like a short ugly piece of pipe. My partner has one, and I have one." He walked several steps towards Mark and stopped. He pointed his flashlight at the trees, and the beam moved down one of the trees to a spot below the tree and cast a spotlight on an empty grave.

Mark stared at the grave, then suddenly he smiled and bent forward laughing. Lifting his head he looked at the stranger and said, "Joanna's playing a practical joke, isn't she. Is she out here too?" He looked around at the darkness, waiting to hear his wife laugh as he yelled into the night "Joanna! Are you watching this?"

He turned back towards the stranger and felt a hand grab his arm and felt a sharp sting in his arm and the stranger's other hand was holding a syringe and giving him a needle. He jumped back full of panic, staring at the needle in the stranger's hand, and spun around and ran into the darkness. His heart was pounding and he was running faster than he had ever run then his feet were in the air and he crashed hard into the ground, his arms stretching in front of him and his fingers clawing at the ground, trying to pull himself forward. He felt his energy leaving his body and slowly stopped moving, only one hand grabbing at the ground in front of his face.

The stranger knelt beside him like he was about to pray, and put the flashlight on the ground. Darkness hid his face as he said, "Relax, it will soon be over. You won't feel any pain."

"Joanna?" asked Mark.

"The grave is big enough for both of you," said the stranger softly. "You will both be together."

Mark said weakly, "I can pay you. I have money."

"We really like you and your wife," said the stranger, and the light from the flashlight revealed a small long box in his hands. He opened the box and took out a surgeon's scalpel that reflected the light from the flashlight. "In a few minutes you will stop breathing, and I'm going to cut out your tongue. My partner and I love human tonge. It's a delicacy we travelled a long way to enjoy. My partner wants me to cut out your wife's tongue. We aren't going to eat your tongues here, we're taking them home with us. Did you ever want to travel in Space? Just think, part of you will be going with us." His hand took Mark's hand and his fingertips pressed against Mark's wrist to measure his pulse. The stranger said gently, "Another minute or two, and it will be all over." He let go of Mark's hand, and Mark was so relaxed and tired he couldn't move as sleep filled his body. He had to wake up from this nightmare.

"It's only a dream, it's only a dream, it's only a dream... thought Mark, staring up into the darkness at the stars and listening to his breaths grow weaker. He had to wake up now. He heard the voice of the stranger in his nightmare say, "Go to sleep Mark. When I get home and I'm chewing on your delicious tongue, I'll remember what you said at dinner about the Buffalo. What would he be doing if he was still alive, discovering a cure for cancer?"

The End.

CHAPTER 3

Three Red Lights

The young man woke up and opened his eyes and realized he was not sleeping in his own bed at home but was in a hospital bed. For one long second he was trying to remember how long he had been in the hospital and why.

And then he remembered everything. Two days ago he had almost been killed when a car running a red light sped in front of his car, but all he could think about was the beautiful dark-haired nurse who had looked after him yesterday. He was staring at the open door of his private hospital room, hoping she would walk in the room and tell him her name.

He got tired of staring at the open doorway, and told himself she might not be working today as he rolled onto his back and stared at the ceiling. He was aware of someone entering his room but when he turned his head to look it was a Doctor. The Doctor looked like he wanted a Doctor to look: Not too young and not too old, with handsome chiseled features and the intelligence and confidence that said he had been at the top of his class at medical school. He lifted a hand and in the hand was an X-Ray. The Doctor smiled and said, "Good news Justin. It looks like you'll be going home today." The Doctor sat on the edge of his bed, showing him the X-Ray of his skull. "We were worried you could have a concussion, but I can't find anything wrong in your X-Rays."

Justin was staring at the Doctor's X-Ray of his skull, and suddenly he smiled and joked, "That would look cool as a poster on my Bedroom wall."

The Doctor stopped smiling, and his face became very serious as he asked, "You do know how lucky you were?" He was worried the accident had taught the young man he was indestructible instead of teaching him to be more cautious. "The police told me they've never seen anybody survive a car wreck like the one you were pulled out of. And you had no injuries, not a scratch."

Justin wore a cocky smile as he announced, "Justin 1, Death 0."

The Doctor half-smiled, playfully swatting the X-Ray against his patient's chest as he stood up and said, "I hope this is the last time I see you at this Hospital." Justin watched the Doctor walk out of the room, closed his eyes, and wished that nurse would walk into the room.

"Are you awake?" asked a pretty female voice, and Justin's eyes snapped open and saw his wish had come true.

"I was just making a wish," said Justin, his eyes memorizing her face so it would always be a perfect photograph in his memory that never faded or changed.

"I hope your wish comes true," said the nurse, forcing a smile but looking a little uncomfortable. She had noticed the way he looked at her, and it bothered her when her friendly nature and love for people was misinterpreted as flirting by some of her patients.

"The Doctor just told me how lucky I was to be alive," said Justin, and he saw the nurse relax and smile sweetly at him. She didn't look much older than 20, and her big blue eyes were sparkling in a beautiful face that was as innocent and curious as a child's.

"What happened?" she asked, giving him her full attention.

"A car ran a red light, I turned my steering wheel so I wouldn't hit it, and my car rolled over several times," he said, the image of that car flashing past him filling his memory. "They had to cut the car open to get me out."

"It sounds like a miracle you weren't hurt," said the nurse, the fingers of her right hand touching something hanging from her neck. Her hand dropped from her neck to reveal she was wearing a tiny crucifix.

"Maybe it was," said Justin. "In the last two years I've cheated death twice driving a car."

"Twice?" said the nurse, her eyebrows lifting and her

fingers returning to her neck to touch her crucifix.

"You're not going to believe this," said Justin, "But I swear its all true. Three years ago my Father was walking home, and as he stepped off the sidewalk to cross the street a car ran a red light and hit him. He lay on the sidewalk dying, and he died as he was being put into the ambulance." He paused, not sure if he she would believe his story. "Witnesses said the hit and run driver who killed my Father was driving a red sports car. It had windows tinted dark so nobody could see the driver."

"I think I remember hearing about that," said the nurse.

"Two years ago I was in my car, waiting for a red light to turn green. It was at night, and very dark, and I was waiting at the same spot where my Father had been when he was hit. The light turned green, and as I stepped on the gas a car appeared out of nowhere and ran a red light. It sped in front of my car and missed my car by a few inches. I hit the brakes and sat there watching that car speed away." Justin paused, hoping the nurse would believe the rest. "The car I saw was a red sport's car with dark windows, just like the one that killed my Dad."

"Oh my!" said the nurse. The nurse sat on the edge of the bed, her hands folded on her lap.

"Yesterday when I had my accident, guess where I was?"

The nurse's big blue eyes stared at him like a little girl listening to a Fairy Tale, her beautiful face believing every word he was saying, and he felt comfortable finishing the bizarre story.

"I was waiting at the same red light where my Father was killed three years ago, and where I could have been killed two years ago," said Justin. "It was the first time I had been back there since my brush with Death two years ago, and it's a quiet night with no other cars on the road. The red light turns green, I step on the gas, and as my car flies forward I see a car flash past my windshield and I hit the brake and turn my steering wheel as hard as I can. Then I woke up in this Hospital."

"The driver hasn't been caught?" asked the nurse.

Justin shook his head no. "There were witnesses. Two teenagers were walking on the sidewalk, but they told police it was so dark they couldn't see the driver." He stared at the nurse, letting the Drama of the moment build until he said as seriously as he could, "They told the police it was a red sport's car."

The nurse's mouth opened in surprise, and her eyes were staring at him like he was the luckiest man on earth. The nurse smiled at Justin and said, "It sounds like you really did cheat death." Suddenly she stood up, and said cheerily, "I'll be back later with your lunch. We can't let you leave on an empty stomach." She started to walk away, and suddenly froze. She turned around and her face was frowning. "I guess you'll never know if it was the same driver who killed your Father and almost killed you."

"I know it was the same driver," said Justin with the certainty of a man totally convinced he was right.

"How?"

"Because all three times it happened it was at night, but the car didn't have it's headlights on."

The nurse was standing as still and silent as statue. Her expressionless face stared at him for several long seconds. "Promise me you will never go back to that stop light again," she ordered, reminding him of his mother when she had scolded him for climbing a tree and falling from it when he was a child.

Justin nodded his head.

He couldn't take his eyes off her as she turned and walked out of the room. The moment she was gone the room felt too empty and too quiet. He slid down under the sheets and turned sideways, the pillow feeling so soft on his face, and closed his eyes. When he opened his eyes he wondered how long he had been asleep, but sunlight was still outside the window.

The room felt strangely cold, and became so cold he felt his body shivering. He hugged himself with his arms and was shaking from the cold. Justin sat up and as his hands began rubbing his arms to warm his body he could see his breath leaving his mouth like cigarette smoke.

Had someone left the window open?

Justin glanced to his left at the window and saw it was closed, then he looked to his right to see if his door was open and he was startled to see the tall thin stranger wearing black clothes. The black clothing looked old fashioned and made his pale skin look shockingly white, almost as white as his short hair. His white face was thin and smooth and there were no lines on his forehead, but his age was revealed by the white hair and dark watery eyes of a very old man.

The tall figure stood there like a ghost, his lips never moving and his eyes never leaving Justin's face. He lifted a bony left hand, the palm of the hand pointing at Justin as the hand lifted two long white fingers. He lowered his hand to his side, and Justin noticed that his own breath was visible in the freezing cold room but he couldn't see the stranger's breath.

The stranger suddenly turned his back on Justin, took two steps, and stopped. He turned around and the cold watery eyes were full of anger as they fixed on Justin. The stranger lifted his hand, again with palm towards Justin, and this time the hand was holding up three long white bony fingers. The angry eyes narrowed to slits as the head shook a silent "No." It was a silent but clear warning that Justin had escaped twice but would not be allowed a third chance.

The man lowered his hand, turned, and slowly walked out of the room. As soon as he was gone the room instantly felt warmer. Justin could no longer see his breath in the air. He pulled back his sheets, put his bare feet on the floor, and walked quickly to the door. He stuck his head out the door, looking up and down the long wide empty hallway.

Justin walked back to the bed and stood there, thinking about what he had just seen. He looked at the window, and walked to the window and looked out. Down below in the parking lot he saw the man who had just been in his room, and he was walking away down the middle of the parking lot. He stopped, walked to his right, and bent down to get in a car. Seconds later at the spot where the stranger stopped and bent down a red car pulled out from the parked cars. The red car sped down the parking lot towards the window, then stopped. Justin saw the car was a red sport's car with darkened windows hiding the driver, and he stepped back in shock from the window. Leaning back towards the window and peeking down he saw the red sport's car was gone.

"Justin, the Doctor said you can leave whenever you want," said a familiar voice behind him. Justin turned around and saw it was the beautiful nurse. He felt foolish wearing the white hospital gown open at the back, and said quickly, "I just had a strange visitor in my room. Do you know who it was?"

The nurse's big blue eyes were surprised, and she shook her head. She smiled and lifted her right hand and the hands fingers wiggled a cute goodbye. She turned and walked towards the door.

"You never told me your name," said Justin.

"Michelle," giggled the nurse as she walked away. Suddenly stopping in the doorway, she half-turned and her beautiful face was smiling as she called out, "Remember what you promised!" The nurse vanished, and Justin walked to the closet and lifted a coat-hanger the held his pants. It was eating him up inside he would probably never see the nurse again.

A few hours later Justin Brand was sitting in a bar. His table was close to the front entrance, and the bar was almost empty. Justin glanced at the left end of the bar where three men sat on barstools drinking silently and politely ignoring each other.

All the other barstools were empty except one on the right end of the bar, where a very pretty girl he guessed was 19 was sitting. She had her back to the long bar and was facing him, twisting back and forth on the barstool. She had squeezed into tight denim shorts that showed off her long beautiful legs, wore a tight red and white striped blouse tied in a knot under her large breasts, and had long brown hair and big brown eyes that kept glancing at him as she twisted on the barstool and sucked on the straw in a glass she was holding with both hands.

His Waitress walked towards him, holding a tray with empty glasses on it, and she looked like she was in her early forties but could easily attract men half her age. She walked behind Justin, leaned down, put his bill on the table, and said, "Take your time, we're open another hour." As she picked up his empty glass she whispered, "She's a lot younger than she looks."

"Why is she in a Bar?" asked Justin, staring into his empty beer glass and a little annoyed the waitress wasn't minding her own business.

"That's the Bartender's little sister, and she's drinking

soda pop."

Justin's darting eyes moved from the young girl at the right end of the Bar so close to where he was sitting to the opposite end of the Bar where the Bartender stood behind the Bar, looking up at a TV set that was showing a Football Game. The Waitress said, "Are you from around here?"

"I used to live a few blocks from here until I was 10. Then my Mother divorced my Father."

"Visiting the old neighborhood?" asked the Waitress.

"My Father was still living in that house until three years ago. One night he was walking home from this Bar, and at the end of the parking lot he was killed by a hit and run driver," explained Justin.

"That was your Father?" said the Waitress.

"Were you working here the night he was killed?"

The Waitress shook her head. "He was a regular, but I hadn't seen him for a few weeks."

Justin's eyes studied her face as he explained, "Not long after my Father was killed, I stopped in here for a drink before driving by my old house, but as I was leaving the parking lot a car ran a red light and almost hit me. I drove away without seeing the house. I haven't been back here until two days ago. I was going to park outside my old house. I came here first, and at the end of the parking lot I was almost killed by a car running a red light."

"That was you?" blurted out the Waitress. She had the

look of a tough woman who had seen it all and heard it all and would be hard to chock, but her face was shocked and she was staring at her customer like he was a ghost. "I can't believe you were almost killed a few feet from where your Dad was killed."

"Did you know him?" asked Justin, not caring much if she did or didn't.

"Nice guy," said the Waitress. "Very quiet. Didn't say much, just sat by himself for hours. After he had one drink, he'd only be drinking coffee. Always left a big tip."

"Last time I saw him, I was 10. My Mother left him because of his drinking. One day when he came home, I saw him walking funny and almost falling over, and I thought he was trying to make my Mom and I laugh. I was laughing, and I started pushing him. He swung a fist at me and I ducked, and he spun around and fell on the floor. I was laughing so hard until I looked at my Mother and saw the look on her face. I'll never forget that look on my Mother's face." Justin paused, and his embarrassed eyes moved away from the waitress's face. "I'd just had my 10th Birthday, and that night my Mother packed our suitcases and we left our house and never went back. I never saw my Father again, or had any contact with him."

"Like I said, I wasn't working the night he was killed," she said slowly. "A few of our regulars, you can tell they are haunted by something. They keep thinking about one moment in their lives that they wish they could change. If they could only take back one stupid thing they said, or did. Or maybe it was something they should have done. If they could only go back to that moment, everything would be different. They'd be living the life they were supposed to live. Instead they sit in here and wish for a second chance."

Justin was only half-listening to the woman and he suddenly said, "You said he didn't talk much?"

"Nothing worth remembering."

She lifted her tray with one hand and the other hand was holding a pen and writing on the Bill on her tray. She placed the Bill near Justin's empty beer glass, and said in a low sultry voice, "No rush." She started to turn away, remembered something, and said, "You may not believe this, but your Father usually sat at this table."

As the waitress walked away Justin was admiring her figure. He turned over bill. Written at the top of the bill was the name Amanda and a phone number. He stood up, took some bills out of his wallet and put them on the table, leaving a nice tip. As he walked past the girl at the bar she bowed her head and lifted her eyes, her eyes following him as she sucked on her straw. Justin walked out of the bar and got in his car. He started his car. His cell phone rang, and he pressed it to his ear. The man's voice on the phone said, "Why don't you stop by? Some of the guys are here, and we want to celebrate you getting out of the hospital."

"Sure," said Justin. "I'll be there in half-an-hour."

"Where are You?"

"I'm at a Bar."

"Where?"

"My old neighborhood."

He pressed the button that ended the call, and put the cell phone on the passenger seat next to him. He drove to the end of the parking lot, and saw the red light. The light turned green, but he sat in his car with his foot on the brake, staring to his right at the spot on the sidewalk a few feet from his front passenger door.

The green stop light in front of him turned red.

His eyes stared at the sidewalk, imagining his dying Father laying there alone, wondering what his last thoughts had been. The light turned green, then he looked up at the green light and took his foot off the brake. As his foot moved to the gas pedal and pressed down something on his right caught his eye. His eyes returned to the spot on the sidewalk and he was startled to see a man lying on the sidewalk. The man looked injured.

Justin's foot stomped on the gas pedal and the car jerked to a stop that pitched his body forward against his seat belt. As his car stopped the color red flashed past his windshield and his eyes looked out the passenger door window and past the man on the sidewalk and saw a speeding red sports car with darkened windows and no headlights on suddenly brake. The car's tires screeched against the road and the car half spun so the car was blocking the street, it's black driver's door window facing Justin.

Justin's cold angry eyes were staring at the black window, and he could feel something cold and evil behind that window staring back at him. For a full minute the other driver stared at him, and Justin knew the face behind that window was the same pale face he had seen in the Hospital that morning. The red car's engine roared several times like a wild animal roaring at something it had been hunting and just watched escape. Then the red car sped off into the darkness.

Justin's right hand scooped up his cell phone from the passenger seat and he dialed 911. A voice answered, and Justin heard the panic in his voice as he said, "There's a man lying on a sidewalk. I think he needs an ambulance." The phone was pressed hard against his ear as his eyes returned to the sidewalk. The sidewalk was empty.

Justin's eyes searched up and down the street but the street was empty and he was all alone. A voice in his phone asked, "Hello, sir. Can I have your name?" Justin Brand's right index finger ended the call. He was staring at the empty spot on the sidewalk where the body had been as he whispered, "Thank you, Dad." His foot stepped on the gas pedal and he turned his steering wheel left, in the opposite direction the red car had gone, and he stepped down hard on the gas pedal.

The End.

CHAPTER 4

No More Chasing A Buck.

The door of the small flower shop opened and the man who stepped out was smiling and holding a dozen red roses. He had a handsome face, short black hair, and was wearing a pin-stripe suit. For a man in his mid-forties he was in incredible shape, and still had the athletic body he had had in college when his passion had for sports had kept him busy playing Tennis, Baseball, and Football. He had surprised everyone by turning down offers to play professional sports, and had taken business courses and gone into Banking. Trading stocks made him rich. Before he was 30 he was a millionaire.

He walked to the silver Ford Mustang, opened the door, and slid into the driver's seat, putting the flowers on the front passenger seat. He left his seat belt off, and drove his car out of the parking lot onto the street. His foot pressed the gas pedal to the floor and the car shot forward down the empty street. He ignored the red traffic light and watched the speedometer show he was doing 85 miles per hour. The silver Mustang was flying through the red stoplights, and he saw his apartment building growing in the windshield until he reached its parking lot.

The car slowed, turned into the parking lot, and drove down a ramp to the underground parking garage full of cars. Taking a small tape recorder out of the pocket inside his suit's jacket, he spoke into the recorder. "Notes for the memoirs of John Crane," he said like a man living a life he had always dreamed of. "This morning I picked up a silver Mustang, I have been driving around the city for hours. wondering if I should propose to my girlfriend Vanessa. I met her in a clothing store while I was shopping, and we haven't known each other very long. I just bought her a dozen roses, and I'm going up to my penthouse to give her an engagement ring."

He got out of the car holding the flowers, didn't lock the car door, and walked to the elevator. He pressed the elevator's button and the double doors opened. Stepping inside, he was starting to feel nervous. What if she said "No?" The elevator took him to the 30th floor and stopped. The doors opened and he walked through the big empty lobby with marble floors and walls and red carpets, and down the empty hall to the door of his apartment. He turned the doorknob and walked in. One wall was glass with a balcony and a breathtaking view of the city, and the large sunken living room was big enough for hundreds of guests. To his right were long coaches facing a large section of wall that was a TV screen. He looked at the back of one of those coaches where she was sitting with her back to him, and all he could see of her was her red hair that she wore long. To her right was a fantastic Bar area, with every kind of liquor bottle imaginable.

John walked quietly to the coach where she sat, sneaking up behind her and placing the flowers on the floor at his feet. He leaned forward and put his hands over her eyes and said, "Surprise!" He kissed her right ear and asked "Did you miss me?" Then he reached down and scooping up the flowers from the floor he placed them on her lap. He kissed her ear again and said, "Read the card."

Vanessa didn't pick up the flowers or say a word, and John said quickly, "I'm sorry they aren't real roses." John's left hand touched Vanessa's red hair, gently stroking it as he said, "Every flower shop I went to didn't have fresh flowers, but these artificial flowers will last forever, just like my love for you." John kissed her cheek, and asked, "Can I make you a drink?" He waited for Vanessa to answer, but she was staring silently straight ahead at the empty TV screen.

John jumped up, and walked to his right to the Bar. He poured himself a Scotch and Soda to give him that extra bit of courage to ask her to marry him. He sipped the drink, and walked to the coach and sat down beside her on her right. He picked up the remote control, pointed it at the massive TV screen covering the wall, and pressed the ON button. Nothing appeared on the screen, and as he used the remote to skip through the hundreds of channels the screen remained blank. He turned off the TV, and said, "There was nothing on my car radio."

He took a drink of the Scotch, and looking into the glass like a fortune teller trying to see the future he said, "Oh, Vanessa, what are we going to do?" He took another drink and put the glass down on the glass table in front of them. Knitting his fingers together, and staring down at his hands, he confessed, "If I didn't have you I would have gone mad. This still feels like a crazy dream. A few weeks ago there were millions of people in this city, and now the city is empty. How could that many people die so fast? I haven't seen one airplane fly over the city in weeks, and the military would have arrived by now. We may be the last two people alive on earth, and I don't know why."

John un-knitted his fingers, and put his left hand on Vanessa's hand. "I don't know how much longer the generators will provide us with power, and we can't live up here in the dark with candles." John sighed, and continued, "I have a cottage just outside the city, and its right on the lake. I just know your going to love it there." He kissed her cheek, and said "If there are any ships out on the Lake, we can see them from the cottage."

John took a deep breath, reached into his suit pocket, and pulled out a tiny black velvet box. He got down on one knee, and opened the box to show her the giant diamond ring. "Vanessa, I know we've only known each other a few weeks, but I fell in love with you the moment I saw you. Please marry me, and I'll make you the happiest woman in the world." John looked up at Vanessa's beautiful, smiling face, and he smiled and asked, "Is that a yes?" He took the ring from the box and slid it on the finger of her left hand, and said, "You'll never be sorry."

John stood up, and said "We better get going while the elevator is still working." He bent down and picked Vanessa up like he was going to do when she was wearing her wedding dress and the wedding was over and he was carrying her into their bedroom. He carried her to the apartment door, bent and turned the doorknob, and his right foot kicked the door open. Carrying Vanessa down the hall to the elevator, he pressed the elevator button and the doors slid open and he carried her inside. This might be the last time he ever rode the elevator down to the parking garage, or visited this building that had been his home for so many years, but as long as he had his Vanessa anywhere she was, that was his home.

The doors slid open and he carried her to the car. Parked next to his silver Mustang was a red Ferrari. "I like the Ferrari more than the Mustang," said John. "Red reminds me of your red hair." He opened the passenger door of the red car, and slid Vanessa inside. She was so light, and was wearing the same black evening gown she had been wearing when he first saw her standing in front of the women's dress department at the clothing store. John had been walking around the empty store, wondering why he was the only one immune from the virus that had killed everyone, and had been looking at all the female manakins wondering which one he should ask on a Date, and then he had seen Vanessa in that tight black evening gown pretending not to notice him.

John closed the passenger door, walked around to the driver's side, and jumped in feeling like a teenager driving his first car for the first time. Reaching over to pull the safety belt over Vanessa, he buckled her in. He turned the key in the ignition and his foot pressed on the gas peddle to make the engine roar. The car sped out of the parking garage up the ramp and into the street.

The car sped down the empty streets though every stop light and stop sign, and raced through the city towards the city's outskirts and the Lake. As they drove he began talking about much his job had been killing him, and now that was all over. "All my life I've been working myself to death," he confessed. "And no matter how much money I made I was never happy. I always needed more. No vacations, No holidays. Wake up early, go to work, chase a buck all day, come home, go to sleep, then wake up and do it all again." He smiled at Vanessa, and said "I'll never have to chase a buck ever again."

After 40 minutes of driving he could see the lake and the cozy one story cottage. The car stopped at the front door of the cottage, and behind it was a cliff that dropped straight down to the beach and beyond the cliff the big blue empty Lake. "Well this is it. I hope you like it," he said to Vanessa. Glancing down at the big diamond sparkling on her finger he was glad he had proposed. He got out of the car, walked around to the passenger side, and opened Vanessa's door the way a gentleman was supposed to. He un-buckled her seat-belt, and as he lifted her out of the car her head hit the car's door frame and her head fell off her body, landing at his feet.

"Vanessa!" he cried, leaning her plastic body against the car as he bent down and gently picked up the plastic head with its beautiful red wig. His hands carefully fitted the head back on the Manikin body. "Why don't you wait in the car while I check the cottage and make sure it's safe." John lifted Vanessa's body back into the car, kissed her cheek, and said, "I promise I won't be long."

John closed the car door, his eyes looking in every direction for any sign of life. He noticed an old grey pickup truck a few hundred feet to the left of his cottage, and it was parked near the cliff. He began walking towards it.

On the drivers' side of the truck the driver's door was open. The open door was pointing at the cliff a hundred feet away. John stood at the open door looking inside the Truck and saw it was empty. His eyes looked at the door pointing at the cliff and imagined what happened, His eyes looked at the ground below the open door and followed the path the driver must have walked towards the cliff. Where the driver's invisible footsteps ended at the cliff was a brown suitcase.

John walked to the suitcase, bent down, and grabbed the handle. He looked at the edge of the cliff and imagined the owner of the suitcase jumping off the cliff.

He tried opening the suitcase but it was locked. His eyes searched the ground around his feet and found a rock that looked big enough. Picking up the rock he began banging the rock against the suitcase's lock. The suitcase opened like a mouth vomiting what was inside, spilling hundreds of green banknotes. At that moment a strong breeze began pushing the paper bills towards the edge of the cliff, and John heard himself shout, "No!"

He let go of the suitcase handle and dropping to his knees his hands began grabbing wildly at the swirling, dancing paper money. Before he could grab more than a handful of bills the breeze turned into a light wind and the money was spreading out as the bills flew and danced towards the cliff. John jumped up and ran ahead of the blowing money to the edge of the cliff, trying to block the money before it went over the edge. The bills blew past him and between his legs and as he turned to catch several bills spinning in the air past him his left foot slipped on the grass at the edge of the cliff. It felt like the grass was pulled out from under him he fell, his hand gripping the paper in his hands.

John saw he was lying along the edge of the cliff, and in the far distance was his red car and he could see Vanessa's red hair. He wanted to call to her, but she was too far away. He knew if he hadn't found her working in that department store, she would still be standing there, frozen in time, never aging, looking so elegant with her upturned right hand forever inviting people to look at the women's dresses, and at night she would be alone in the dark. At least he had rescued her and brought her to the cottage, where she might be safe.

He felt his body very slowly sliding over the edge. His right hand let go of the money and shot out and grabbed at the grass so he could pull himself away from the cliff, but the grass tore in his hand and as his right hand squeezed the handful of torn grass he rolled sideways a few feet down the cliff and stopped. He looked at the money in his left hand was squeezing, and reluctantly opened his fingers and watched it float away.

Slowly, very slowly, he turned his body so it was vertical with the cliff and he was facing up, but as his hand reached for a rock to pull himself upwards he was suddenly sliding downwards, his body twisting and hands clawing and grabbing at the cliff and then his hand grabbed something soft and his body jerked to a stop. He looked up and his right hand was gripping a shrub that grew out of the face of the cliff.

John was breathing hard and looking up at the spot where he fell, his eyes measuring the distance he would have to climb, then he forced his eyes to glance down to see how far he could fall. It was over a hundred feet from the bottom of his shoes to the sand and big rocks below. Closing his eyes he looked up. He opened his eyes. The climb up looked almost impossible but he had to try. He called out in a loud clear voice, "God, if I'm the last man alive on Earth, you can't let me die like this!"

Waiting for his prayer to be answered he stared up at

the edge of the cliff, and saw one of the bank notes appear and float down, and as it danced down the rocks towards his face it stopped a few inches above the shrub he was holding. Pulling on the shrub with all his strength he felt his heavy body inching upwards, and suddenly he was filled with hope. He pulled hard again and the shrub moved, coming out of the ground, its roots starting to break. One or two more pulls on the shrub and he was going to slide down and fall to his death. His angry eyes stared at the dollar mocking him.

John Crane closed his eyes.

The End.

CHAPTER 5

Cupid Wore A Mask

"Julia's not working today?" said the man standing in front of the counter in the record store.

The customer was wearing a mask because of the Covid virus, but even a mask covering the lower half of his face couldn't hide he was handsome enough to be a movie star. He looked younger than his 27 years, had brown eyes and short brown hair, and a tall, athletic body. He was trying hard to hide his deep disappointment that his favorite member of the staff wasn't in the store.

The young woman behind the counter was wearing a white mask that had musical notes on it, and her soft voice said through her mask, "My sister hasn't been feeling well."

"Sister?"

"I'm Jennifer London, and Julia and I share an apartment. I just started working here today."

"I'm Christopher Newman."

"Oh! You must be the customer Julia told me about!" said Jennifer, her eyes smiling as they matched his appearance to her sister's description of him. "She can't believe you both love all the same music she does!"

"I haven't seen her for weeks, and I was worried," said Christopher.

"It's nothing serious," Jennifer said quickly.

"Good," said Christopher. "Tell Julia I said Hello."

"Oh I will!," said Jennifer excitedly, her eyes smiling like she had been hoping he would say that.

Christopher walked out of the store feeling depressed. He knew he liked the girl a lot, but the sadness he felt was so deep he realized for the first time he was falling in love with her.

A week later Christopher was standing in the kitchen of his apartment, opening the fridge door and looking inside when the cell phone in his pocket began softly ringing. He reached into his pocket, put the cell phone to his ear, and heard Julia's voice ask, "Is this Christopher Newman?"

"Yes," said Christopher.

"This is The Oasis Record Store calling," said Julia's far away voice. "The Jazz album you ordered is in. It's $24.99."

"Thank you, I'll pick it up today," said Christopher. He

heard the long seconds of silence as Julia waited, then she hung up.

Christopher quickly put on a light coat, rushed out the door without checking to see if he locked it, and he stood outside his apartment next to a bus stop waiting for a bus. It was a short bus ride to the Mall where the record store was, and when he walked inside he went straight to the counter.

Julia's sister was standing behind the counter doing nothing, and to her right the store manager was talking to a customer. Christopher walked up to Jennifer and said "I just got a call from the store. You have a Jazz album I ordered."

Jennifer looked at Christopher and nodded, bending down to look under the counter and pulling out an LP sealed in plastic. She handed the LP to Christopher. Christopher was holding the LP with both hands like it was a book and reading the back of the cardboard sleeve. He heard Jennifer say, "You got the call from Julia. She's back at work but had to leave."

Christopher's eyes lifted from the LP to the young woman's face, and saw her embarrassed eyes dropping their gaze from his face to the counter. She looked eager to tell him more, and was forcing herself not to say anything. Christopher's eyes returned to the back of the LP, and he said, "I had taking the plastic wrappers off the albums. It makes the covers look like glossy photographs. Usually I leave the plastic on and just cut open the side so the record can slide out."

He heard Jennifer laugh. "Julia does the same thing."

Christopher handed cash to Jennifer, and she handed him back the change. As he walked away he heard Jennifer call after him, "I'll tell Julia you said Hello."

For the next two weeks Christopher didn't visit the record store or the Mall it was in, then one afternoon he decided to pop into one of the Mall's clothing stores and buy some shirts. He bought the shirts and was walking out of the Mall's main entrance when he saw Julia walking into the entrance, her eyes staring at the ground in front of her. As she was walking past him suddenly she looked up and saw him, her masked face startled.

Christopher stopped walking and Julia froze, standing like a statue in her navy blue coat and black pants and black boots. Christopher saw her eyes were red and looked like they had been crying.

"Long time no see," he joked.

"I've missed you," said Julia, her mask not able to hide her tortured face and sad eyes as she stared at the floor, not wanting to leave.

Christopher sighed. "Would you have dinner with me?"

Julia's eyes widened in surprise. She looked happily excited but afraid, and stood there unable to speak or nod yes or shake her head no. Her pretty voice was so low it was almost a whisper as she said through her mask, "OK."

Christopher smiled and felt like a great weight had been lifted off his shoulders, and he wished he could hug Julia and just stand here silently holding her. He asked her if she'd like to go to a small Italian restaurant close to the Mall, and she looked like she was in a trance as she nodded.

"This evening, at 7 'O Clock?"

"OK," said Julia in a tiny voice.

Christopher walked away, stopped, looked back, and Julia was still standing there like a statue. He turned and walked out of the Mall, and had never felt so happy. Christopher walked home, searched through his LP collection for the LP's he and Julia loved the most, and put the first one on his turntable. As the last LP was playing, he went into his bedroom, put on a dress shirt and tie, then put on a jacket and watched the record needle lift from the spinning vinyl disc. Turning off his stereo he walked to his door and looked at his watch. He had plenty of time to get there and wanted to be early.

Inside the small Italian restaurant Christopher asked for a table facing the restaurant's big front window. He sat down at the small round table that was perfect for two people but could sit four, and took off his mask. A waiter wearing a mask appeared, and Christopher smiled and said, "I'm expecting a friend at 7 PM."

Picking up the menu and glanced at the pictures of food and drinks, then gazed at the door and imagined her walking in and sitting down. She could finally take off her mask and he could see how beautiful her entire face was for the first time. Looking at his wristwatch he saw the time was 20 minutes to seven.

Christopher kept glancing at his watch until it was 7 PM. When he looked at his watch and it was 7:30 PM he heard the waiter's voice behind him saying, "Your friend isn't coming?" He knew the waiter had guessed it was a woman and he had been stood up, and he asked the waiter for a cup of coffee. Christopher sat drinking cups of coffee until 8 PM, then he paid the waiter and left a big tip and walked out of the restaurant.

The next day Christopher was standing in front of his record player looking at the shelf above it that held his favourite albums, and his hand reached for an LP and plucked it from the shelf. He stared at the cover art made glossy by the plastic wrapper he had left on the cardboard sleeve, and started to slide the record out of its sleeve. He stopped, pushed the record back into the sleeve, and returned the album to the shelf.

His cell phone rang inside his pant's pocket. Holding the phone to his ear he heard a voice that sounded like Julia's sister Jennifer say, "This is Oasis Records. We have a record you ordered."

"I didn't have any records on order," said Christopher.

"It has your name on it," said Jennifer.

Christopher closed his eyes and said, "OK."

An hour later as he walked into the record store he didn't see Julia behind the counter or in the store. He saw three members of the staff, and two were busy talking to customers but Jennifer was behind the counter looking through a stack of LPs. Christopher said to her, "You phoned and said I had an order?"

Jennifer didn't look at him but she reached under the counter and put an LP on the counter in front of him. She turned her attention back to the stack of LPs and continued examining each one, putting the ones she looked at in a new pile.

Christopher saw the little yellow piece of paper stuck to the cover of an LP he hadn't ordered and wouldn't have bought. He said matter-of-factly "I didn't order it." He saw Jennifer's eyes glance at the LP and she said quickly, "We must have made a mistake." Her eyes returned to the record pile and she lifted another LP from the first stack of LPs. She was acting like she had promised someone not to talk to him, and was angry she had agreed to be silent.

Christopher turned, and as he was walking away from the counter he heard Jennifer's voice say quickly, "Sometimes she likes to go to the park and sit on a park bench to watch the sun go down."

Christopher stood outside the Mall staring in the direction of the park. As a Taxi rolled towards him he lifted a hand to make the Taxi Driver stop. The Taxi braked and he got in the passenger side. "I'd like to go to the park," he said to the Taxi Driver. Fifteen minutes later the Taxi let him out at the park. He walked towards the water. Walking along a path between the edge of the lake and a row of 10 park benches facing the lake, he saw all the benches were empty except for the last bench a hundred feet away. The figure on that bench was sitting alone. He walked a little faster, and saw the lone figure was a woman.

The woman on the bench was staring across the lake at the orange sunset, and she was wearing a mask. When he could see the woman was Julia he stopped walking. The urge to turn around and walk away was strong, but not strong enough. He walked to the bench, and sat down next to Julia. His eyes never left her face but she wouldn't look at him, and she began crying.

"Why are you crying?" asked Christopher.

"I'm falling in love with you," said Julia.

Christopher heard himself say, "You have a strange way of showing it." His words turned Julia's face towards him, and her sad wet eyes were begging him to forgive her. He heard himself say, "I've already fallen in love with you." His words seemed to wound her and she quickly looked away. After a long silence she asked, "Would you love me if I wasn't beautiful?"

"I don't understand."

She slowly lifted her hands to her face, and her hands were trembling as they very slowly removed her mask. He could only see her right profile but was shocked at how beautiful she was.

Christopher said, "You're the most beautiful woman I've ever seen."

She turned her face towards him and her embarrassed eyes waited for his reaction. On the left side of her face a short, deep scar started at the corner of her lip and ended at her chin. She said quietly and without any bitterness or self-pity, "When I was 5, my neighbours' dog attacked me. I had plastic surgery, but my parent's could only afford one operation."

"I still think you're the most beautiful woman I've ever seen," said Christopher, and he saw how badly she wanted to believe him. "I know what your job is, but I never told you what I do," said Christopher. "I'm a Fire-fighter. I've only had one close call, and I thought I was going to die. I woke up in the hospital, and it took me a long time before I could look in the mirror." His hands removed his mask, and she saw how fire had melted part of his lower lip and left his chin badly scarred.

Julia's face was an expressionless mask as her eyes studied his face. Her sudden smile was the most beautiful smile he had ever seen. Her hand reached out quickly but gently to touch the scars on his face, then her hand reached for his hand. Gazing deeply into each others eyes they held hands as the setting sun darkened their faces, the night painting over their faces to hide the burns and scars like an artist to erase what their eyes had already erased.

The End.

CHAPTER 6

The Book Lover

"Yes we're still open" said the second-hand bookstore owner into his cell phone as he stood behind the counter of his store. He was in his early 40's, tall and slim and full of energy, with brown eyes, thin brown hair cut short and combed straight back, and a friendly familiar face that often made customers ask, "Have we met before?"

The voice on the phone said, "I have a lot of books I have to find a home for. Can I bring some by today?"

The store owner's large blue eyes were looking at his wrist watch on his left wrist, and he said "We close in 90 minutes, and I can't stay open late." He heard his caller hang up, and was putting his phone down on the counter next to the cash register when he heard the store's front door open.

Three young woman he hadn't seen before walked into the store and began looking around. Today his customers had all been young people, and that made him happy because it proved wrong all the predictions bookstores were dying out.

For the next hour and 15 minutes he stood behind his counter pricing books and had to keep stopping because it was surprisingly busy. He counted 44 young shoppers --31 of them buying at least one book-- before his watch told him it was 15 minutes until closing. The store was empty and he was thinking about closing 10 minutes early when the door opened and a short elderly gentleman walked in carrying a leather bag heavy with what must be books.

"I spoke to you on the phone an hour ago. About finding a home for my library," said the old man. He looked like he had been ill, and his face was sad.

"Oh yes!" said the man behind the counter. "I'm Robert Town, the owner of the store."

"Frank Cuthbert," said the old man. He lifted his leather bag onto the counter, and opened it. His sad eyes watched the man behind the counter take out a dozen books one at a time and quickly examine each one. They were expensive looking collector's editions of classic fiction writers, and he knew the man behind the desk would want all of them."

"My wife has been making me get rid my private Library, but I have over 200 books left. Those are the ones I want to keep the most, but she insists they all have to go."

"Why is your wife doing that, if you don't mind me asking?"

The old man stood there looking helpless, his face embarrassed as he tried to find the words to explain.

The store's owner had such a natural liking of people he never had to pretend to be interested in the strangers in the store, always giving them his full attention, but he was forcing himself to keep eye contact with the saddest eyes he had ever seen.

Was the old gentleman desperate for cash to pay his rent, or a medical bill, or buy food?, wondered the store owner, as he hoped the customer wasn't going to start begging and crying.

"I don't usually pay cash," the owner said softly. His face was serious, his large blue eyes watching for any sign this was life-or-death conversation for his visitor.

"I don't need the money," said the old man, looking at the floor and guessing how this might look to the stranger behind the counter. He had a lot to say but was a private man with old school manners and was not going to force this store owner to listen t his life story.

"How many books do you have to sell?" asked Frank, becoming his old friendly self and bursting with curiosity about why a man who showed so much pain about selling his books was doing it if he didn't need the money.

"I have a small library, literature mostly. Some History. Over 500 hardcover books that took me a lifetime to collect. I was an English professor at a small college."

"How many books in your library are you selling?"

The old gentleman's lips moved but he couldn't speak

for several long seconds, then he managed to force out the words, "All of them."

The bookstore owner's eyebrows lifted, then he frowned and asked "May I ask why?"

"I promised my wife," said the old man.

"She wants you to get rid of all your books?" blurted out the owner, eager to hear the man's story even if he had to keep the store open late.

The old man looked defeated, and had to let go of what remained of his pride before he could admit the truth. "Well, its like this," he began, trying to find the courage to admit the sad truth. "My wife told me that when I'm gone, she doesn't want to be burdened with having to get rid of all my books. So she wants me to take care of it now."

The store owner looked down at the floor, embarrassed and wishing the man hadn't told him. He tried to picture the man's wife, wondering what a woman like that looked like and sounded like, but his mind was a blank.

"500 books?" said Frank, thinking to himself what was the largest number he could possibly buy.

Frank said quickly, "My library used to have 500 books, but I've been giving them away to old students of mine, the mailman, sending them as Birthday gifts to friends and relatives. I thought when I got down to the last 200 or so, the ones I couldn't let go, my wife might change her mind." Frank's face and voice let the store owner know Frank's wife had not changed her mind.

Robert watched Frank's sad eyes stare at his books on the counter and it seemed he was talking to them instead of the store's owner as he said, "I could live another 10 years, maybe more, so I don't know what I'll do when the last books are gone."

Robert leaned forward and said, "Usually only give store credit, but the last thing you need are more books," he said lightly, trying to make the old man smile. "If all 200 of your books are as fine as these, I'll pay you $3,000 dollars for the collection.

Frank nodded, and asked "Could you come and pick them up?"

"What time is good?" asked Robert.

"Tomorrow afternoon."

Robert had an idea he knew the old man would like. "I won't pick up all 200 books tomorrow, I'll make several trips over the next few weeks."

Frank smiled and suddenly looked ten years younger. Knowing all his books wouldn't be gone tomorrow was the best news he could have expected. He wrote down his address and phone number on a piece of paper, handed it to Robert, and walked to the door. As he opened the door he paused and turned and his eyes returned to the counter, giving his books a final look and saying a silent goodbye.

The door closed and he was gone.

Robert looked at his wristwatch and saw his new friend hadn't kept him here one minute past closing. It was exactly 5 PM.

The next afternoon Robert Town was in his car parking in front of the house that matched the address on the paper Frank had given him. He walked to the door and knocked and a moment later the door opened and a woman in her 50's was standing in the doorway. She was medium-height, and wore a white dress with a flower pattern. Her hair was dyed ink black and her plain, stern face had quick eyes that quickly evaluated Robert. "You're a little early" she said, and he wasn't sure if it was criticism or a compliment.

"Mrs. Cuthbert?" asked Robert. She didn't answer, instead giving him a look that asked who else could she be?

Robert stepped inside, and Mrs. Cuthbert pointed to her right at several boxes on the floor, and he guessed there were about 50 books in them.

"I asked the garbage men for boxes," said the woman. "And the maid put the books in the boxes."

"Can I see the rest of the books?" asked Frank.

Mrs. Cuthbert stared at him, then reluctantly nodded. She looked down at his shoes, waiting. Robert removed his shoes and Mrs. Cuthbert led him down a hallway to a small study that had couches and chairs and bookshelves. The once full bookshelves were almost empty, and in one of the chairs Frank sat with a blanket over his lap, his eyes closed.

"Before I made him get rid of those books, his health was a lot better and he didn't sleep as much," said Mrs. Cuthbert. "I honestly thought he was putting on an act, so I'd change my mind." Her stubborn, hard chiseled face and stubborn cold eyes advertised the fact she rarely, if ever, changed her mind.

Robert walked to the bookcases, glancing at the 150 books still on the shelves. He walked back to where Mrs. Cuthbert was standing, and said to her "I'll come back tomorrow."

The next day he arrived at the same time, and again when he knocked the door opened and Mrs. Cuthbert had been standing there waiting for him. He walked inside and looked at the spot where the boxes had been yesterday. He saw more boxes holding another 50 books.

"How's Frank?" asked Robert.

Mrs. Cuthbert said, "Frank was too sick this morning to get out of bed. Same time tomorrow?"

Robert nodded, dropping his gaze to the floor and feeling sorry for Frank as he listened to the sound of Mrs. Cuthbert's shoes on the polished wood floor as she was walking away.

"Day three," said Robert Town as he parked his car in front of the familiar house and made his third visit. He looked at his watch and he would be on the doorstep exactly on time. He knocked on the door expecting it to immediately open but nothing happened. He knocked again, waited, and knocked again. Finally the door opened. Mrs. Cuthbert said, "I was on the phone with the hospital. Frank was taken to the hospital last night, but their bringing him home tonight."

"I'm sorry to hear that," said Robert, walking into the house and looking where he knew the boxes would be. Same number of boxes, same number of books. "Another 50 books," he said wistfully, trying to brighten the cold environment in the house. "I'll be back for the last 50 tomorrow. Say Hello to Frank." He bent down to pick up the first box, and the sound of Mrs. Cuthbert's shoes were fading down the Hall.

"Last trip," said Robert as he sat in his parked car outside the Cuthbert's home. He hated the idea of seeing Mrs. Cuthbert again, but after today he'd never have to see her again. He knocked on the door and the door immediately opened. Mrs. Cuthbert let him in. The last 50 books were in the boxes on the floor.

"How is Frank," asked Robert.

"He's in his study, and he's awake," said Mrs. Cuthbert. "He wants to say goodbye."

Robert removed his shoes, and followed Mrs. Cuthbert down the Hall to the study. She remained outside and walked away, and Robert Town saw Frank sitting in the same chair where Frank had been sleeping during Robert's first visit. Robert smiled down at Frank, and Frank tried to smile as his watery pale blue eyes said Thank

You.

Robert took a cheque out of his pocket and handed it to Frank, who had trouble lifting his arm. His fingers pinched the cheque and put it on his lap, but he didn't look at it. "We agreed on $3,000, but I added a little more."

"I have a gift for you," said Frank, and he reached under the blanket and was holding out a thin hardcover book for Robert. Robert took the book and read the title: 'The Book Lover," by Frank Cuthbert. It had a white cover, and Frank was turning the pages and glancing at a few sentences.

"It's self published," said Frank weakly, "And that's the only copy. Its about how much I loved collecting my books. It doesn't have any illustrations." Frank's right hand gestured for Robert to lean closer. As Robert leaned closer, Frank lowered his weak voice to a whisper and said, My wife doesn't know about it." Frank lifted a finger to his lips to let Robert it was their secret, and Frank was smiling like a naughty child.

"I promise I'll keep it," said Robert, feeling like he might cry.

"I know," said Frank.

Robert's eyes moved from Frank's face to the now empty bookshelves, and he wondered if he would ever see the old man again, or possibly get a phone call. "It was wonderful meeting you Frank, you take care and good luck!" Robert walked to the study's doorway, turned back to wave at Frank. Frank looked so small and fragile in the big chair, but he looked comfortable.

Robert walked to the front door and saw it had been left open for him, and he bent down to pick up the first box. He put Frank's self published book in the box so it wouldn't get damaged, and carried the box to his car.

Robert parked in front of his closed bookstore, unlocked the door, and carried in the boxes of books. He put the boxes behind the counter, and took Frank's book out of it's box. He walked to the back of the store and out the back door, then walked up the fire-escape to the apartment above the bookstore where he lived. He sat down on a couch and began reading Frank's book, and couldn't stop reading. By the time he finished reading he was ready for bed, and he looked at the book's simple cover and thought "This could have been a best-seller." Feeling a sudden nagging urge to phone Frank and tell him how much he loved his book, he took a card from inside the book that had Frank's name and phone number on it. Squinting at his writing on the card, Robert began pressing the numbers on his cell phone, but as his finger was about to press the phone's call icon he hesitated. It was late and Frank was probably asleep. Robert put down his cell phone and thought "I'll phone him tomorrow."

In the morning Robert woke up early, got dressed, made a cup of coffee in his small kitchen. As he walked down the stairs from his apartment above the bookstore to the bookstore's rear entrance, he was carrying a cup of coffee and Frank's book. Inside his bookstore, he unlocked the front door, turning the Closed sign hanging inside the door to OPEN, and walked behind his counterto phone Frank.

Staring at Frank's book as it lay on his counter, he held his cell phone and pressed the numbers of Frank's phone number.

"Hello?" said a voice that sounded like Frank's wife.

"Mrs. Cuthbert? Hello? Town Books, Robert Town speaking."

"Yes?"

"Could I speak with your husband?"

"Frank died last night," said Mrs. Cuthbert.

"I'm so sorry," said Robert.

"Frank had a cheque in his wallet from you, for $3,400. He didn't tell me about that money."

"I thought you knew," said Robert. He waited for Frank's wife to say something, but all he heard was angry silence.

"Well, the money will pay for the funeral," said Mrs. Cuthbert, and she abruptly hung up.

Robert put down his cell phone, and picked up Frank's book. "It could have used a few illustrations," he said softly, wishing he had phoned Frank last night. He began flipping through the pages, and as he saw the last page of the last chapter his body froze and he was staring in shock. On the page on the left was the last page of the last chapter, and the page on the right that had been blank last night when he finished the book was an old fashioned ink sketch of a man who looked exactly like Frank sitting in a chair and study identical to Franks. Frank's face was smiling and his empty bookshelves were full again.

Robert's right hand started to touch the page with the drawing of his friend, but his fingers froze, afraid to touch the illustration that had not been there when he finished the book. His eyes were suddenly frightened and right hand jerked away from the page. He let go of the book and as it fell he turned away from it his elbow knocked over his coffee cup on the counter, spilling the coffee down the back of his counter onto the floor.

Robert stared at the book as it lay near his feet, and as the puddle of coffee on the floor inched towards the book he bent down and carefully picked it up, placing it on the counter. He walked to his store's front door, turning the sign hanging in the door's window that said OPEN to CLOSED. He walked back around the counter and sat in his chair, silently staring at Frank's book as it sat on the counter.

The End.

CHAPTER 7

The Strap

The teacher was standing in front of her classroom, her back to her desk and the wall with the chalkboard and the wall clock above it. That wall clock was being stared at by almost all the 13-year-old boys and girls in the room as they sat at their desks waiting for the recess bell to ring, and the room was so quiet the ticking sound of the clock could be heard by the teacher and the students in the front row.

Seconds before the bell was going to ring, the teacher announced in a calm, clear voice "No recess this morning class." She watched the children's faces change from expectation to misery, then added, "This morning one of you wasn't paying attention, so all of you will stay in your seats when the bell rings." Her eyes fixed on the good-looking boy with short blonde hair who was falling asleep at the back of the room, and she smiled as her voice sang out sweetly "Except for you Scott."

She had timed it perfectly and seconds later the bell rang loud like a fire alarm, and Scott opened his eyes and suddenly wide-awake and full of energy he jumped out of his chair and walked quickly out of the room.

The Teacher was thin with a thin face that was almost pretty, and had just turned 27 but looked like she was in her mid-thirties. The beautiful large brown eyes in her pale face were the thing most people remembered about her. Her eyes were ignoring the rows of sad faces and were only interested in the cigarettes in her purse as she looked inside her purse to make sure it had her cigarette lighter.

Satisfied the children would sit frozen like silent statues during recess, she turned and walked out the classroom's only door desperate for a cigarette, her high heels clicking on the tiles echoing in the hallway as she walked to the nearest exit door and opened it. Outside the door one hand quickly plucked a cigarette from the pack and put it in her lips as the other hand flicked the cigarette lighter and touched the flame to the tip of the cigarette. A light breeze blowing towards her made her turn her body to face the door behind her, and she saw her reflection mirrored in the door's square window.

The woman she saw reflected in the glass was almost 30 but still pretty enough to turn the heads of a few young me, and her short dark brown hair look seductively black. As she studied her face in the door's window the door opened and a female teacher her age appeared holding a cigarette and book of matches and said, "Hi

Joan."

"Hello Heather."

"I had to cancel recess again for my grade 8 class," said Joan as she puffed on her cigarette.

"Except for Scott," said Catherine.

"He comes from a good family," Joan said matter-of-factly.

"You've never met them," said Catherine.

"Scott's family has the biggest house I've ever seen, and his uncle's house is almost as big," gushed Joan.

"Thank's for teaching my class yesterday," said Heather, and her face was beaming with good news. "I had the teaching job interview yesterday morning, and when I got home yesterday afternoon they phoned and told me I got the job."

Joan looked a little disappointed, and said, "We just met, and your already leaving. I was hoping we would be friends."

"Its less money, but I can't wait to leave."

"Why?" asked Joan, looking a little hurt.

"The Teacher you replaced told me something before she left, something about Scott Bishop and his Brothers."

"You don't believe rumors do you?" asked Joan, her face surprised and a little disappointed in the other woman.

"She wasn't the only one who told me," said Catherine. "When I got this Teaching job four months ago, the Teacher I replaced visited me at home. She told me she was leaving because one of her student's, a 12-year-old girl, came to her crying about what Scott and his brothers were doing to her in his parent's mansion. How they got her drunk then all took turns. They told her if she told anybody, they would kill her dog." Heather's eyes studied Joan's face and saw nothing was going to convince her it was true.

Joan's stubborn face stared at the horizon, waiting patiently for Catherine to drop the subject and never mention it again.

"The Teacher you replaced also talked to the girl, and told me the same story," said Joan.

"Why didn't they go to the police?" asked Joan.

"They did," said Catherine.

"And?"

"Scott's Uncle is the police chief."

Joan looked at the other Teacher, hating her for confiding something so terrible but wanting to hear more. Catherine lowered her voice and spoke fast, the words spilling out, "The police did nothing, and both Teachers started getting phone calls threatening their lives. The Teacher I replaced quit, and the one you replaced started getting pulled over in her car by the police every week and getting speeding tickets. I was driving with her once when she got pulled over, and she wasn't speeding." Catherine took several puffs on her cigarette, her eyes studying Joan as she whispered, ""That same Teacher told the poor girl she's lucky she didn't get pregnant. And do you know what the girl said?"

Joan looked up from the ground where she had been staring at the cigarette she had just smoked, her eyes tired of the conversation but curious. Catherine's face was angry as she forced out the words: "She said, I can't get pregnant. They don't do it to me the way that makes babies."

Joan stiffened and her face blushed, and she was wishing she could forget what she had just been told. She stared at the cigarettes on the ground and asked, "Where's the girl now?"

"A few days after she told her teacher that, her parent's suddenly put a 'For Sale' sign in front of their house. A few days before they moved, Scott showed up at their house with a BB Gun and shot the girl's dog. The police asked Scott what happened, and he said the dog was going to attack him. The police wanted the Vet to lock up the dog and put it down, but when the parent's dropped their charges against Scott the police let the dog go." Heather finished her cigarette and dropped it on the ground. "Thanks again for covering for me," said Heather, grinding the cigarette under the toe of her shoe.

The next morning at 8 AM Joan was standing at the front of her class, her eyes glancing at all the faces of her seven-year-old students as they sat silently at their desks waiting for her to speak. "I have an announcement, class," sang out Joan in the pretty voice she saved to give the class good news. "We have a new girl in the class named Emily, so please make her feel welcome!"

Joan's face was beaming with a big welcoming smile as she looked at the front row where the pretty little girl with brown hair and blue eyes sat. The child had an angelic face, wore a beautiful, expensive looking blue dress, and her smiling face was trying hard not to giggle as she was looking to her left and right at the girls sitting next to her. She was so happy to be in the class and so delighted to be making new friends it made Joan feel as good about being a teacher as she had when she graduated teacher's college and been handed her diploma.

After the class was over, Emily jumped up and was walking with her two new friends when Joan called out, "Emily, could you please stay a minute?"

Emily walked back to where Joan was standing and Joan sat down in the chair behind her desk. "What a pretty dress. It looks very expensive."

"Mama and Daddy bought it for me for my last Birthday."

"The Principal told me what happened to your parents, and I'm so sorry."

Emily stopped smiling, and she said to the floor, "I miss Mama and Daddy every day."

"I know you do, sweetheart," said Joan, and she wanted

to give this little angel a big hug. "I was told you love to draw with crayons."

"Oh yes!"

"Are you going to be a famous artist?" teased the teacher.

The little girl blushed and giggled and looking shyly down at her hands said "I don't know about THAAAAT!" The compliment really tickled her and she couldn't stop smiling.

"Are there any artists in your family?"

"My Mama used to be an artist. She taught me to draw."

"You think about her when you draw, don't you."

"I feel like she's sitting next to me when I colour," said the little girl.

"What else do you like to do?" asked Joan, giving the child her full attention.

"I like to play piano, but I'm not very good yet," admitted Emily, her small face frustrated. "

"Did your mommy and daddy have a piano?"

The child nodded.

"Did your mommy play piano?"

The child nodded and said, "Daddy wanted me to have piano lessons so I could surprise Mama."

"Did you know the school has a piano?"

"Yes!" said the excited child. "The Principal showed it to me. I can't wait for my music class!"

"That's so sweet," purred the teacher tenderly. "Who looks after you now?"

Emily smiled proudly as she announced, "I live with my Grandaddy!"

"Does he have a nice house?"

"Oh yes! He has a big Trailer," said Emily.

"Trailer?" said Joan, her smile vanishing.

Emily nodded. "I have my own room!" declared the child with a big proud smile, looking and sounding like she was a princess living in a palace.

"Well Emily, I have a lot of work to do," said the Teacher. Emily smiled sweetly and ran out of the room. Joan looked in her purse for a pack of cigarettes and stood up. She counted the cigarettes. Her next payday seemed a long way away, but cigarettes were a luxury she had to fit into her budget.

Outside the school's side entrance, Joan stood in the smoking area enjoying how much the unlit cigarette felt between her lips. As she lit a match and held the flame to the cigarette, inhaling the smoke slowly and closing her eyes, she heard the door behind her open.

"Hi Joan."

"Hello Michelle."

Michelle lit a cigarette and said, "I'm going to miss Catherine."

"So am I."

Michelle's face brightened. "What do you think of that new girl, Emily."

Joan exhaled smoke, studied her cigarette, and said, "It's a shame about her family," said Joan. "One day she's living in a nice house and wearing beautiful dresses, then a drunk driver kills her parents she's in a Trailer."

"Is your mother still asking you why you aren't married," asked Michelle.

"The last time she phoned, she was asking if the Principal was married and how old he was," said Joan, a smile playing on her lips as she imagined herself and the Principle as a couple.

Michelle laughed. "Maybe if he lost 40 pounds and was 20 years younger and we were stranded together on a desert island," laughed Michelle, her comedic timing perfect as she paused and added, "and I was drunk." Both women laughed, and were silent as they finished their cigarettes.

A week later Joan was sitting in her classroom during recess, and the desks were empty except for the desk in the front row where Emily sat with crayons drawing a picture. Joan said to Emily, "You know the school doesn't have money for everything we need, so the Teachers buy crayons and paper with their own money."

Emily looked up from her desk with a big smile on her

face, and said "Miss Carter, I have a surprise for you." Emily jumped out of her desk and handed her Teacher the paper she had been colouring. Joan put the paper on her desk and stared at the picture of a child holding hands with an adult woman who had brown eyes and dark brown hair and was wearing a green dress just like the one Joan was wearing.

"Is that you and me?" asked Joan.

Emily nodded and said, "If you ever feel lonely you can look at that and remember we are friends."

The word "Lonely" stung Joan and she was thinking of all the times her Mother nagged her about not having friends or a boyfriend or a husband. "What makes you think I'm lonely?" asked Joan, trying to hide her embarrassment.

"Isn't everybody lonely sometimes?" asked Emily with big innocent eyes waiting for an answer.

"Well thank you Emily," said Joan, and a moment later the bell rang ending recess and the children poured back into the classroom. For the rest of the day Joan felt embarrassed that people might think she was lonely and were feeling sorry for her. When the bell rang at the end of the day Joan watched the children race out of the room, looked at an Apple on her desk she hadn't eaten at lunch, and walked quickly to the smoking area. Michelle was finishing a cigarette and said, "Have you heard Emily play piano in her music class? She has a gift for playing. I just walked past her classroom and heard her playing. She's the last kid in the school, and

I'm afraid she'll miss her Bus."

"Have a good night Michelle," said Joan, taking her last puff of her last cigarette.

"You're always the last one to leave," joked Michelle, and she walked towards the parking lot.

Joan walked back into the school, and as she stepped into her classroom her eyes immediately noticed the Apple on her desk was gone. She walked quickly down the hall to the school's back entrance, and as she opened the door and stared at the school bus's full of children start to drive away she saw the small figure of Emily running towards the one school bus waiting for her. Joan's eyes narrowed to angry slits and she felt the anger boiling inside her.

The next afternoon during the school's final class, Joan stood outside Emily's music class with the Principal. As they listened to Emily play piano, the Principal walked into the class and Joan waited outside. The piano music stopped and the Principal walked out with Emily. Joan and the Principal walked down the hall with Emily between them, and they took her into the Principal's office and closed the door. The Principal sat down at the chair behind his desk, and turned his chair so he could face Emily as Joan stood guard behind the child.

"Emily, do you know why you're here?" asked the Principal.

Emily shook her head "No."

"Are you sure?" asked the Principal.

"Emily," said Joan coldly, putting her hands on the child's shoulders, "Yesterday when you were the last one in the school and everybody was on the school buses, my Apple on my desk was stolen."

The Principle studied Emily's innocent face, and saw she still didn't understand why she was here. "Emily, do you know what happened to that Apple?"

Emily shook her head "No", and Joan's angry hands tightened on Emily's shoulders.

The Principal opened a drawer in his desk, took out a thick leather strap, and handed it to Joan. Emily turned and looked up at Joan, still not understanding what was about to happen. Emily was so small that when he stood behind her he looked like a bear standing on it's hind legs, and suddenly his big powerful hands clamped on Emily's small shoulders so she couldn't run. Joan reached down and grabbed Emily's right arm, twisting her arm so the palm of her hand was facing up. As Joan held Emily's arm with her right hand the strap in her left hand swung down hard on Emily's palm and made a loud CRACK that filled the room. The child opened her mouth wide in a silent scream and started struggling, her eyes bulging with terror and pain. Joan swung the strap down again.

The CRACK! of the strap and the child's scream filled the office.

"Are you sorry you did it?" shouted Joan, lifting the strap and ready to bring it down again.

"Did you do it?" asked the Principal, hoping the child would confess so the punishment could stop.

Emily shook her head "No" and her eyes begged for mercy.

"Stop lying!" screamed Joan. "I spend my own money on you children, and you pay me back by stealing from me! And lying!" Emily closed her eyes to shut out the horror, and as she started crying Joan brought the strap down again on the hand that was already swollen red with a loud CRACK!

"That's enough, Joan," said the Principal as he let go of Emily, and the child fell on the floor, curling up in a fetal position, crying hysterically. Her body was shaking and her good hand was trying to cover her red swollen hand as she moaned, "Daddy, Daddy, please help me! Their hurting me!" Her eyes closed tightly as she called out, "Daddy don't let them hurt me."

"Give me the strap, Joan," said the Principal, holding out his huge open hand. Joan's hurt face and disappointed eyes stared at the Principal, and she tried to reason with him. "But Tom, she hasn't confessed yet." Joan's eyes burned with rage and she looked like an avenging angel doing the work of God as she spat out the words, "Or said she was sorry!" The Principal's hand inched closer to Joan. Her shoulders sagged and she looked defeated as she reluctantly put the strap in his hand. He dropped the strap in the open drawer of his desk, and as he closed the drawer Joan walked out of the office towards the smoking area. All she could think of was the taste of a cigarette.

The next day, during the children's lunch break, Joan was standing in the smoking area, sharing a cigarette with Michelle. "Don't you love Teacher's pay," said Joan, trying to laugh.

"I knew about the pay," said Michelle. "But Teacher's College didn't tell me I'd have to share cigarettes," said Michelle.

Joan chuckled and nodded, and her eyes fixed on Michelle as she said, "You're the only teacher not giving me dirty looks. Even the Principal is avoiding me."

"They don't think we should use the strap," said Michelle.

"I was just doing my job," said Joan.

Michelle's face looked troubled as she stared at Joan, and she quietly asked, "Why are you so certain Emily did it?"

"I know it was her."

"Because her grandfather is poor?" asked Michelle, her eyes narrowing and face full of suspicion.

Joan made a face and rolled her eyes. She looked at her cigarette a few seconds, and said, "She's the only one in the class not afraid of me."

"Really?" asked Michelle. "What about Scott Bishop? Thirteen years old, starting High School next year, and he's a walking drug store who does whatever he wants.

He falls asleep in my class, and the Principal won't do anything about it. Do you know what Scott calls his gang? The 'Masters of the Universe.'"

Joan's pinched face hardened. She said quickly, "Scott doesn't have to be afraid of me, he's from a good family."

"His family think they own this town and everyone in it, because they do," said Michelle.

"You sound just like Heather," said Joan, making a face.

Michelle frowned. Her cold eyes were studying the other woman like she was seeing who she really was for the first time. "I didn't become a teacher so I could teach children their place in an economic class system. Neither did Heather."

"I'm teaching them right from wrong, and people from good families don't have to be taught that," Joan said sharply, talking to Michelle like she was one of the children in Joan's classroom.

The door opened and Heather walked out.

"We were just talking about you," said Michelle to Heather.

Heather was wearing her coat and carrying a box full of things that had been in her desk. "The Principal said I could leave early today" said Heather.

"I was hoping you could stop by my place for a drink," said Michelle with a playful pout.

"I'd love to Michelle, but I start my new job tomorrow, and it's a long drive," said Heather. She looked at Michelle and said, "I'm really going to miss you. I'll give you a call tonight when I get to my new apartment."

"Have a safe trip, Heather," said Joan.

Heather smiled at Michelle and said, "Michelle, I need to talk to Joan in private."

Michelle smiled and said, "Sure Heather. I'll be waiting for your phone call." Michelle opened the door and went inside, leaving the two women alone. The second the door closed Heather put the cardboard box down on the ground, and moved closer to Joan. Her voice was as cold as her eyes as she said, "The Principal told me Emily's grandfather pulled her out of school. And he told me what happened in his office. When she got home her Grandfather drove her to the Hospital. The Doctor's said Emily's hand has nerve damage."

Joan stiffened, angry that Heather was making her sound like the villain instead of the victim. Joan's voice rose as she asked, "If I hurt her that much, why was she in school this morning?"

"She came to say goodbye to her friends," said Heather. "Her grandfather waited for her in his car while she said goodbye to some of the children. He told me nobody asked his permission to punish his granddaughter."

"So now I'm the bad guy?" asked Joan, her head tilted at an angle and eyes cursing Heather.

Heather's right hand flew up a slapped Joan's face. Joan didn't flinch or react in any way. Michelle was trying to control her temper, forcing herself to speak in a low calm voice as she said, "When I saw that little girl this morning I didn't recognize her. Then I saw the big bandage on her hand and realized it was her. I've never hated anybody as much as I hate you." Michelle's hand flew up and slapped Joan's face as hard as she could.

Joan was standing as frozen and expressionless as a clothing store Manakin as Heather bent down and picked up her cardboard box and walked away. Joan walked back inside the school, and sat in her classroom marking papers. Her eyes kept looking at her cheap wristwatch. She must have looked at her watch a hundred times before the last bell rang and the children ran to the school buses. Joan stood up and walked to the smoking area, dying for a cigarette. As she stood outside the side door she looked down on the ground at the cigarette butts, and had to resist the urge to pick one up and light it.

The door burst open and Michelle appeared smiling triumphantly holding up both hands and both hands had a cigarette. "Look what I found!" Handing one of the cigarette's to Joan's eager hand, Michelle said, "See you tomorrow!" and started walking towards the parking lot. She stopped, half turned, and her face was grinning at Joan as she called out, "You're always the last one here! They'll have to make you Principle!"

Joan had a little smile on her lips because it was the first compliment anybody had given her in a long time. She lit another cigarette and watched Heather walk to her car, get in her car, and drive away with a goodbye wave.

Joan finished the cigarette, dropped it on the ground, and walked back to her empty classroom in the empty school and was feeling lonely. She was standing behind her desk, wondering what her mother would say if they made her the school's principle. Suddenly aware somebody was behind her she quickly looked over her shoulder and relaxed. "Oh it's you Scott," she smiled. "It's just you and me."

"Yeah," muttered Scott. His feet shuffled softly from behind her to the side of her desk, and as she reached for her apple his hand shot forward and grabbed it. He lifted it to his mouth and took one bite and dropped the Apple into the wastepaper basket.

"Oh Scott!" she said sweetly, "That was my lunch!" She frowned at the apple in the waste-paper basket and asked, "Scott, were you here any days this week after the school busses left?"

"Maybe," said Scott.

Joan leaned on the desk, and her shoulders sagged as she closed her eyes a few moments. Her eyes opened and she stated, "You would have had to walk home, and that's a long walk."

"One of my Brother's picked me up in a car."

Joan frowned and said, "But none of your Brother's are old enough to drive."

"My uncle is police chief," said Scott.

"Scott honey, did you eat my apple Wednesday after school?" asked Joan.

"No," said Scott.

Joan relaxed and sighed, the terrible feeing she might have punished the wrong person gone. She felt guilty for asking the question, then realized Scott might tell his parents she had suspected him of stealing. She looked over her shoulder and smiled her prettiest smile and said, "Scott, honey, I know you would never do that."

As she looked back down at her desk she heard Scott say, "I said I didn't eat it, I didn't say I didn't take it."

Joan froze and stopped smiling. She frowned and asked, "Why would you do that?"

"It was a joke," said Scott.

"Oh, it was only a joke!" smiled Joan.

"Yeah, said Scott. "I wanted to see who you would blame."

Joan's left hand touched her forehead, and she said as gently as she could, "Scott, you shouldn't do things like that. You come from a good family."

"I do what I want," said Scott.

Joan stood up, arranging things on her desk as Scott moved behind her and stood closer than he should have. Their bodies were almost touching. Glancing at her wristwatch she said, "Oh, look at the time!" Scott pressed his body against her body and she froze. His body and hands shoved her forward against the desk then his hands were on her shoulders forcing her to bend forward until her breasts were pressed flat against the top of the hard desk. She felt a hand lift the back of her skirt then the same hand slid her tiny black thong down her legs to her knees. Her ears could only hear the Tick...Tick...Tick of the clock high up on the wall behind her then the terrifying sound behind her of his zipper being pulled down.

One of his hands covered her mouth and she screamed into his hand before she felt the stabbing pain. She heard him moaning loudly then swearing then praying then he stopped moving and sighed loudly. His hands let go of her and she heard the sound of a zipper being pulled up.

"Got any smokes?" asked the bored voice behind her.

Joan saw his hands grab her purse from the top of the desk and pour everything inside it onto the desk. He put the purse back on the top of the desk. The only sound in the room was the ticking of the clock and his soft footsteps walking away. Joan was standing outside her body, watching herself stand up and pull up her thong. She watched herself sit down behind her desk and reach for the papers on her desk. The woman she was watching looked and moved like a robot, copying her routine with robotic precision, imitating perfectly how she lifted the stack of papers and tapped their bottom edges on her desk to make a neat stack, then reaching out for the report cards.

As Joan watched herself she wanted to cry, and she squeezed her eyes shut, When she opened her eyes she was back in her body, sitting behind the desk, feeling nothing and her mind empty, and she reached for the stack of report cards. Glancing at each card to make sure she had graded them all, she came to the last card and saw the C grade she had written in red felt marker. It was the lowest grade in the class, and her eyes moved down from the C to the name Emily Brown. She dropped the report card into the garbage pail beside her desk and it sat next to the Apple.

The End

CHAPTER 8

Nebuchanezer's Other Dream

Vienna was one of Europe's most beautiful cities during the day but at night many visitors would say it was the most beautiful city in the world.

One of the few visitors who could ignore the city's beauty in daylight and at night was walking alone on a cold autumn night below the city's streetlamps on one of it's longest streets, his shoes unpolished and his pant legs too short and overcoat too big. His brown homburg hat fit, and below it was a pale round face with a little moustache and large patient intelligent eyes. If any of the people walking past him had noticed him, they might have guessed he was a Bohemian musician or artist.

A musician or artist would have noticed the city's beauty, but the only beauty the visitor could see and feel around him was the beauty of the city's women. His eyes glanced at every beautiful and pretty face walking past him, and they were all being escorted by gentlemen because a young lady would not have been out walking alone after dark. Suddenly the most beautiful face and figure he had ever seen appeared under the streetlamps like an actress stepping onto the spotlight on a stage, and she was holding the arm of a young gentleman she was strolling with, but they only had eyes for each other and as she walked past him he found himself wondering if it was scientifically possible to calculate the odds if he would ever see her again.

Her face was still filling his memory when the street sign he was looking for interrupted his calculations and his mind returned to the job he had to do. Turning down the street he walked for a few minutes before turning down another street and hearing shouts and laughter from a café where most of the tables were empty. Around one table at the café sat a group of soldiers in their bright dress uniforms, holding bottles of champagne and lifting their glasses to drink a toast. Walking past the café he saw a newspaper on an empty table and stopped, picking up the newspaper to eye the front page, then his eyes fixed on the date. The new century was already 5 years old but the world still had soldiers.

From the café it was a short walk to the street sign that told him to turn left and at the end of this short dark street he could see the tall fence and behind it the dark shape of the big building. He looked at his watch and saw he was on time. Walking towards the gate he saw behind the gate the dark shape of the guard.

The gate opened just wide enough for him to enter,

then quickly closed and he heard the rattle of keys in the guard's hands. He followed the guard to the building and again heard the sound of keys then the door opened and there was electric light behind the door. Walking through the door he could see the guard's large round pleasant face with its patient eyes.

"Hello Albert," said the guard. "Can I take your coat and hat."

He took off his coat and hat and handed them to the guard, who hung them on hooks on the wall as he said, "Any luck finding a job today?"

The visitor shook his head.

"Too many teachers, not enough students. And if we have a war a lot less students," said the guard matter-of-factly.

Near the door they had entered the guard had an old desk pressed against the wall and above the desk a naked lightbulb hung from a long cord, it's bright light shining on a shelf above the desk heavy with books and on the top of the desk where a violin lay.

The visitor walked to the desk and his eyes glanced at the titles of the books then dropped and fixed on the shiny violin on the desk. "We have something in common. How well do you play it?"

"I haven't had any complaints," smiled the guard.

"Tomorrow I leave for home, so I won't be bothering you again."

"I've enjoyed your visits this week, we get so few visitors," smiled the guard. "Just look at our empty visitor's book,"—his hand gestured toward the big book on a small table by the entrance—"nobody wants to be seen visiting an insane asylum."

"You have been a good host," said the visitor.

The visitor's gaze lifted above the desk to the framed coloured illustration of the empire's old emperor, and next to it a big framed map of the old man's vast empire that covered the middle of Europe, and across the top of the map the words 'Austro-Hungarian Empire'.

The guard looked up at the framed picture with some affection, and said "Our dear old Emperor Franz Joseph has been on the throne longer than most of his subjects have been alive, and I'm afraid when he dies our empire will go with him. All these nationalities in our empire, speaking 15 different official languages, and for generations we have had peace and prosperity, but if our emperor dies tomorrow we fall and break apart like Humpty Dumpty." The guard smiled at his visitor and looked a little embarrassed as he said, "Forgive me Professor, you did not come here to listen to me talk politics. I get so few visitors, and I miss having these kinds of conversations."

The visitor's face became very serious, and his voice was low and angry as he said "I have grown up and gone to school in Germany, so I have seen nationalism at its worst. I believe nationalists should be locked up in here, before they bring the world crashing down on our heads." The guard's two hands slapped the top of his desk, and he said loudly, "Well professor, I hope you find what your looking for. Of course I might be able to help you, if I knew what you are looking for.

The visitor looked at the guard's honest face and thought a moment, then said, "I work in a patent office where I have very little work, so I have time to write my scientific papers." His eyes returned to the books on the shelf, and he continued, "No one wants to read my papers because they contain theories I haven't been able to prove, and because I don't discover scientific theories the way other scientists do."

The visitor saw his honesty had surprised and impressed his host, so he kept talking, his eyes moving to the violin on the desk. "I was playing Mozart on my violin when I remembered that Mozart's great rival Solieri ended his days in an asylum like this, and some people considered Mozart himself a little mad. I began thinking about the fine line that can exist between genius and madness, and since I was coming here to look for a job I decided to also visit an asylum."

"Well you won't find any Mozart's here," said the guard.

"Experiments take time."

"Time you are wasting," said the guard's big friendly face, trying to make his point without offending his guest.

The visitor gazed at the guard, and began speaking like a teacher to a young student. "I have met many scientists, from all over the world, and some of them have met our world's greatest scientist. Do you know what he told them?"

The guard looked like the perfect student, his ears hungry for everything his teacher was saying. The guard sat like the perfect student, seeing and hearing nothing but his teacher. "He believes," said the visitor slowly, "That tiny people live in our brains, operating our brains like machines in a factory."

The guard laughed, a big belly laugh that made his body shake, and his right hand slapped the arm of his chair.

The visitor waited for the guard to stop laughing, then said "He is our greatest inventor. He has invented things that once seemed impossible, and now he is trying to build a machine to communicate with these people he believes live in our heads."

The guard laughed again, certain his guest was pulling his leg, and his eyes were challenging the visitor. "Has he invented anything I would know?"

The visitor's eyes answered by moving to the lightbulb hanging above the desk.

The guard's face knew at once the name of the inventor, and his face grew serious as he realized his guest was not pulling his leg. The visitor saw the surprise on the guard's face as he realized who they were talking about and understood his guest was perfectly serious. He put himself in the guard's place, and knew the man didn't believe the story and was thinking of an excuse to ask his guest to leave. He said quickly, "Of all the inmates here, can you think of just one who stands out from the rest?"

The guard shook his head, his bored face unable to separate any of the mad faces that filled the rooms in this building. His expression instantly changed as he remembered one inmate who did indeed seem somehow different from all the others. "Well there is one..." murmured the guard, thinking out loud. He looked at his visitor and asked, "Are you a religious man?"

"No."

"Have you heard of King Nebuchanezzer, the King of Ancient Babylon?" asked the guard.

The visitor didn't answer.

"It is a story in the Old Testament. The King had a strange dream, and sent for a prophet to interpret his dream," said the guard, reaching for one of the books on his bookshelf. Pulling out of the shelf a black leather Bible, his fingertips were turning the pages quickly. "King Nebuchanezzer of Babylon dreamed he saw a great statue of a man with a head made of gold, the chest and arms silver, the belly and thighs iron, and the legs and feet were iron mixed with clay. A huge stone not cut by the hands of man struck the feet of the statue and destroyed it. Then the stone grew into a mountain that covered the world."

The guard closed the Bible and put it back on the shelf, and continued, "When the king could find no one to interpret his dream, he sent for the prophet Daniel, and Daniel told the king the four parts of the statue were four different kingdoms, and Babylon was the first kingdom with the golden head. In time all four great kingdoms would be destroyed by God, and God's kingdom was the mountain covering the world."

"You have an inmate who is the prophet Danial?" asked the visitor.

"Better!" declared the guard. "He thinks he's the King, and he's had another dream about the end of the world!" The guard put the Bible on his desk, stood up, and led his guest down a long corridor. The guard stopped at a door and pulled keys from his pocket, sticking one into the doors lock and pushing open the door.

Sitting in the middle of the floor, hugging his knees, was a man with a long black beard and black hair as long as a womans. The face behind the beard might have belonged to a man in his 40s. His eyes were sunken deep in a face that was thin and pale. He seemed unaware anybody was in his cell. The visitor smelled the stink in the cell, and looked at the dirty wall behind the inmate and the dirty floor. The guard's face was embarrassed as he looked down at his dirty shoes and mumbled "We try keeping it clean."

"Why do you think he's different?" asked the visitor.

The guard's face turned right towards the wall behind them that the inmate was facing, and the visitor turned right and to face the wall and his eyes widened. Every inch of the dirty wall was covered from top to bottom with mathematical formulas scribbled with white chalk, looking like a giant version of a blackboard in a science classroom.

The visitor walked to the wall, his eyes glancing everywhere he saw numbers. His eyes and brain were taking in all the numbers as he heard an unfamiliar voice behind him ask, "What is your name?", and he answered in a low voice "Albert."

The visitor abruptly turned to face the inmate sitting on the floor, and saw the guard was just inside the doorway.

"We have been waiting for you," said the man on the floor.

"Why?"

"We once had a dream, and God sent us his prophet to interpret that dream. The prophet told us the dream meant my kingdom would fall, and I would lose my throne. Everything the prophet said came to pass." The inmate's sunken eyes accepted his fate, and he sounded and looked like a man who knew what it meant to rise to great heights and lose everything. "We have had another dream, and we have waited for another prophet to come."

"What did you dream?"

The inmate's right arm lifted and his right-hand's index finger pointed at the wall covered with white numbers. He was pointing at a spot low on the wall, and the visitor's eyes followed the pointing finger to the spot on the wall. Kneeling down his eyes darted from one math equation to the next until one series of numbers and a letter jumped out at him:

E=MC2.

"Will we be king again?" asked the inmate.

The visitor looked over his shoulder and saw the inmate's body stiffen, and he began crying, his mouth opening to let out loud sobs. His right hand lifted and became a fist and he punched his face. The guard rushed from the doorway to the inmate and grabbed the inmate's arm to stop him beating himself.

The visitor's eyes returned to the wall and his hand slowly reached inside his overcoat, pulling out a handkerchief. Pressing the handkerchief to the wall he rubbed the spot he couldn't stop staring at. His handkerchief smudged the numbers on the wall, making them impossible to read.

Putting the handkerchief back inside his overcoat, he stood up quickly and his eyes never looked at the inmate again as he walked to the doorway and stood there waiting for the guard. The guard pulled the door shut, his keys already in his hands and the right key poked into the doors lock.

From behind the door came a scream that sounded like the scream of a trapped and tortured wild animal driven crazy from pain. The guard thrust the keys into his pant's pocket and both men walked down the corridor to the guard's desk.

"In all my years here, I have never heard a scream like that," said the guard, his big round face afraid.

"May I?" asked the visitor as he reached for the violin

on the desk, picking it up and the violin bow. Tucking the violin under his chin he touched the bow to the violin strings, and very gently brushed the strings with the bow to make the violin sing out its first sad notes. A familiar piece by Mozart filled the room, and the bow putting more pressure on the violin strings produced a sound so loud and beautiful that it merged with the inmates haunting scream still stuck in his ears and the scream and music merged and then there was only the long beautiful sound of the violin. When the music stopped the scream was gone and he put the violin and bow on the desk.

"Did you find what you were looking for?" asked the guard.

"Yes," said the visitor. He took his hat and coat from the hooks on the wall, putting on his hat and coat as the guard opened the door. The guard walked him to the gate, opened the gate, they shook hands, and the guard said "You are always welcome here."

The guard shut the gate and locked it, as he had done thousands of times before, but this time it was different because suddenly he felt terribly alone and afraid to go back into the building.

Back at his desk he stared at the violin then glanced towards the entrance and noticed the visitor's book. It had not been signed by his guest during his visits. The guard walked quickly to the front door, pulled it open, and looked out into the night. His guest was gone. Closing the door he walked to the small table displaying the visitor's book, opened it, and took the pen lying below the book. Slowly he wrote on the empty white page his visitor's name: Albert Einstein.

CHAPTER 9

Comrade Monster

Georgi Lupov woke up and opened his swollen eyes and saw he was still in the prison cell and it was not all a bad dream.

He lay on his back on a hard iron cot with no mattress or blanket or pillow staring up at the grey ceiling and turned his head and saw the grey walls and terror filled his aching body.

How could he be a prisoner of Russia's secret police in Moscow's Lubyanka prison, his face and body bruised from police beatings, when only three weeks ago he had been hundreds of miles from here running one of the biggest factories in the Soviet Union.

He had been a man going places, the boss of hundreds of workers who built tractors, thinking of the day he would meet the great boss himself, Comrade Stalin. How many times he had imagined this meeting, rehearsing it over and over in his mind so if it happened he would not make a fool of himself.

Lupov was too exhausted to lift his head, but he found the strength to slowly lift his right arm so the fingers of his right hand could touch his swollen face. His fingertips touched his numb lumpy face, and he was glad the cell had no mirror or anything shiny enough to let him see his face. If he didn't see what those fists had done to his face he would not cry or shit his pants. Those jailers would love to see me cry or shit my pants, thought Lupov.

A noise at the cell door made him turn his head towards the metal door, and he stared at the door as he heard the sound of keys turning in the door's lock and the door opened. Two big men stood in the doorway, one holding the doors keys. Lupov thought the two men looked and acted like machines, and he remembered the machines in his factory. A machine could only be controlled by the man who pushed its button, and Lupov was helpless as the two machines reached out, grabbing his arms and pulling him off the bed then dragging him towards the door and out into the corridor.

Lupov was a big man, with big shoulders and a big chest and big belly, but he felt like a small weak child as the machines pulled him down the short corridor towards a closed steel door.

Behind the steel door was the man who pushed the machines' buttons, and the machines opened the door and dragged him inside. The room was small and almost empty, with only a square table with two chairs. Sitting in one chair facing him was a man wearing a black leather coat and black leather cap who looked like he was in his mid-thirties. His hair was black as shoe polish and his thin face was so white it made his dark eyes look black. On the table in front of him was a stack of papers and beside it an open file folder. Behind him was an unpainted wall and on the wall above his head a framed coloured photo of the boss.

The boss had an angry but patient face, the eyes of a wolf, thick jet black hair and a big black moustache, and he was staring to his right, into the future, imagining a world where all his enemies were in prison or dead. Like the God the priests and old women still believed in, the boss was everywhere and he was in the room. And his voice would fill the room as soon as the pale man behind the desk opened his mouth.

"I am Comrade Malik," said the man behind the table. "You have been here in the Lubyianka prison for three weeks, and every day you refuse to confess your guilt."

"My arrest was a mistake," said Lupov.

"The Party does not make mistakes," snapped Comrade Malik, sounding like a man who used this phrase a hundred times a day. With both hands he lifted the thick stack of papers on his table, holding them in front of his chest, and declared: "Each one of these papers is the death sentence for workers at your factory you accused of being traitors." He lowered the papers back on the table, and said sarcastically, "So many traitors."

"It's a big factory," said Lupov, and he heard a snort of laughter behind him from one of the two machines.

His interrogator's cruel black eyes glanced at the guard

behind Lupov who had laughed warning him not to do it again, then he suddenly stood up to let the prisoner see how tall he was. He towered above the short plump prisoner slouched down in the chair, and leaned forward trying to look even more threatening and rested both fists on the desk. Staring down at Lupov he looked and sounded like an angry schoolmaster talking to a child as he asked, "Who told you to accuse all these workers of being spies?"

"You know who."

"I want names."

"I was following orders."

Comrade Malik's eyes narrowed to slits. "Orders from who?"

"Comrade you know who," said Lupov.

"Orders from who?" hissed Comrade Malik, his black eyes locked on his prisoner's face.

"We had quotas to meet," answered Lupov.

"Orders from who?"

"The one who gave us quotas."

"Orders from who?"

Lupov's eyes answered by glancing up at the face in the framed picture, the picture of the great Stalin. Stalin, who never slept and was everywhere, always watching and listening, living in every village and town and city in the Soviet Union, and he was in this room now filling Comrade Malik with his power and suspicion and cruelty, whispering encouragement in his ear.

"Traitor!" shouted Comrade Malik.

Lupov spoke slowly, telling his interrogator what they both already knew. "The Party told us if our factories did not meet production quotas, it must be because our factories were being sabotaged. Every time the Party raised production quotas, some workers complained the quotas were impossible. They asked how can a machine that only makes 20 parts an hour make 30, then 40, then 50 an hour? Every time I turned in these traitors I was congratulated by the Party."

Comrade Malik's thin pale face turned red. His face looked like raw meat and his eyes bulged with rage, his thin lips unable to speak. He looked at one of his giant goons standing behind Lupov's chair, and the giant stepped forward quickly and Lupov felt a big fist crash into his ear and almost knock him out of his chair. Lupov swayed in his chair, trying not to fall, dizzy from the blow and feeling warm liquid trickling from his ear down his neck.

Comrade Malik looked down at his open folder and was reading silently, and kept reading as he said "Your file says you are from a farm. Your parents and their parents were farmers." Comrade Malik's small dark eyes lifted from the file and fixed on Lupov. "Our revolution was made by the workers, not farmers. It was our factory workers who made the revolution by going on strike, then defending our revolution by fighting in our army. Workers of the world unite means nothing to farmers.

They only want bigger farms so they can make more money by exploiting the workers."

"I am a factory worker," said Lupov.

Comrade Malik's left hand moved to the stack of papers on the desk, his left hand's index finger tapping the top of the papers. "I ask you again Lupov, how could so many workers be spies?"

Lupov said calmly, "If they were innocent, why were they all executed? The Party doesn't make mistakes."

Comrade Malik spun around with his back to Malik, like a doll suddenly blown by a great wind. He stood there frozen, facing the wall. He faced the wall a long time. Comrade Malik slowly turned back to face his prisoner. He was scowling, straining to project all the authority given to him by the state. His bosses wanted confessions and names, and he had to meet their quotas to prove he was doing his job. There was always another comrade ready to take his job and if that happened he, Malik, would be sitting in that prisoner's chair, but unlike this fool he would have no illusions about being saved.

Comrade Malik sighed and eyed his prisoner, his patience exhausted. "We can do this the easy way, or the hard way," said Comrade Malik matter-of-factly. "The hard way takes longer but in the end you will still sign the confession, because everybody does. Everybody."

Lupov's stubborn face and stubborn eyes told the interrogator he would never sign the confession.

"You are thinking if you confess you will be executed," said Comrade Malik, "but you are more use to us alive. Give the Party what it wants, and the Party will show mercy. Someday you could get your old job back."

Lupov stared at the wall and said nothing.

Comrade Malik lowered his voice and spoke slowly, letting every word sink in, "We have already found you guilty. Only your punishment is being decided. Do you understand?"

Lupov's stubborn eyes stared at the table top.

Comrade Malik saw that being tough was getting him nowhere, and the prisoner might drag this out for days, weeks, maybe months. He wanted the signed confession today. He became calm and businesslike, talking to the prisoner almost like a friend. "Look, its very simple. You have to show us you are willing to improve before we can show you mercy. This—" he pointed at the stack of papers—"can all be forgotten."

Lupov sat like a statue, ignoring his interrogator's poor attempt to act like an old friend trying to make up after a big argument.

"You big men are always the first to crack," said Comrade Malik. He looked past Lupov and nodded, and Lupov felt like the arms of a bear were hugging him. His lungs and right arm were being crushed but his left arm was free. He was struggling to breathe as he saw the other man who had been behind him step in front of him and grab his free left hand.

"You are right-handed, and we need your right hand to sign the confession," explained Comrade Malik. "So my friend is going to use his hammer to smash each finger of your left hand, then all ten of your toes, then your balls, and if you still aren't begging to sign the confession, he will start on your right hand, and I will stick a pen in your mouth and you will sign." The moment Comrade Malik stopped talking Lupov felt the machine gripping his left wrist slam that hand flat on the table and a hammer came down on the little finger and Lupov screamed. The hammer came down again on the finger next to the little finger and Lupov screamed louder and kept screaming, then he began crying, sobbing uncontrollably.

Comrade Malik stood up and walked around the table to Lupov, placing a sheet of blank paper on the table in front of him. The big arms hugging Lupov relaxed, then let go, and Lupov felt the machine behind him lift his right hand and put it on the desk. Into his right hand was poked a pen by Comrade Malik. "The confession you sign is blank," explained Comrade Malik, his voice warmer, "so we can lessen the charges against you if we see you can be rehabilitated."

Lupov slowly got his fingers around the pen, and scribbled his name on the bottom of the blank paper. He let the pen drop onto the table, then as his red eyes lifted to fix on Comrade Malik he felt and looked like an exhausted dying Bull staring up at the Matador about to plunge a sword into him. Lupov heard himself groan through the pain, "I know your real name. It is Comrade

Monster."

Comrade Malik had what he wanted and had lost all interest in his prisoner, and Lupov felt like he had suddenly become invisible and no longer existed. No hint of his fate came from the thin cruel man who turned and walked out of the room holding his precious piece of paper.

Lupov's left arm was burning with pain as the two machines pulled him out of the room and pulled him down the corridor, their shoes clapping briskly against the tile floor, and Lupov realized they had made a mistake and turned the wrong way, taking him farther from his cell with each step. When he was back in his cell he would wait and hope and there was a chance they would send him to a Labour Camp. Ten or twenty years in a Labour Camp in Siberia would be Hell, but he was young and strong and anything was better than a bullet in the back of the neck.

"Your going the wrong way," mumbled Lupov, but the machines didn't stop.

At the end of another corridor they opened a door and took Lupov inside, into a long narrow room where dozens of people of all ages and sexes were taking off their clothes or were naked. The machines were taking off Lupov's clothes, stripping as easily as two adults taking the clothes off a child. As soon as he was naked they left the room.

Lupov saw several guards in leather coats and black leather worker's caps holding revolvers appear and start herding some of the naked people through a doorway, and one of those guards looked at Lupov and gestured with his revolver for Lupov to join the people leaving the room.

Lupov felt naked bies pressing against him as they were herded into the next room, and looking over the tops of heads he saw a row of eight wooden doors along one wall. Facing the eight doors were eight guards in long leather coats and leather caps, and in the large space between these eight guards and eight doors eight naked people walked quickly towards the doors and stood facing the doors. The eight guards lifted their arms and Lupov saw they were holding revolvers and aiming at the people facing the doors.

"Fire!" shouted a voice.

All eight revolvers made one deafening noise and the naked people facing the doors dropped. Lupov looked at the front of the line he was standing in, and saw the back of the head of a small man in a uniform and cap of the secret police, and he was counting off each group of 8 naked people who would walk to the 8 wooden doors and face the doors as the 8 men in leather coats and leather workers caps lifted their pistols and aimed.

BANG!

All eight pistols fired at the same moment making one sound and the eight naked bodies facing the eight doors dropped like eight sacks of flour hanging from string suddenly cut.

Lupov's nose smelled only the gunsmoke hanging in

the air and as he looked past the naked bodies standing in front of him he saw the line ended where a small middle-aged man in a smart police uniform and cap was standing. He looked and acted like a friendly but tired conductor on a streetcar who was gently controlling the movement of passengers boarding and leaving his streetcar. "Come along comrades, we don't have all day," said the small man, his eyes never looking at the faces as he was counting the next group of naked bodies who were walking past him towards their place in front of the doors.

Eight more bodies faced the eight doors and the eight executioners lifted their arms at the same moment and aimed their pistols.

"Fire!"

Again eight pistols made one deafening Bang! and all eight naked bodies facing the doors dropped like flesh-coloured sacks. The eight men with guns were like eight machines, and their guns like parts of those machines, their revolvers chambers snapping open to be fed more bullets and snap shut.

From the left side of the room a group of men dressed like factory workers walked quickly to the eight naked bodies on the floor, and each body was being lifted by its arms and legs by two men, their blue overalls wet with sweat and blood. The carried the bodies back to the left side of the room, vanishing through a door.

The small man in charge of the line was standing on Lupov's left, his eyes looking only at the floor, and Lupov asked him "Uncle, where did they go?"

The small man stared at the floor and spoke fast. "Large steel hooks lift the bodies on a hoist up to the street, where truck's are waiting to take them away to be cremated."

Lupov heard the boy in front of him start sobbing loudly, and saw his body shivering and his hands hanging at his sides shaking. The boy was the only naked body in front of him. They were at the front of the line.

A forgotten memory popped into his head: he was a boy and it was before the revolution when churches and priests were everywhere and Lupov was inside a massive church, surrounded by smoke pouring from pots hanging from chains carried by priests, the pots swaying slowly at the end of their chains, and a priest with a great grey beard and burning dark eyes stared at Lupov and his hand made the sign of the cross as he and the other priest's chanted. The priest's burning dark eyes stared at Lupov and the priest's mouth was moving but Lupov heard only silence. The priest kept talking, his face stern, his eyes angry, and Lupov tried reading the priest's lips and tried to guess what he was saying. The smoke from the pots carried by the priest's filled the air in front of Lupov's face, and Lupov could see it all as clearly as a bright colour photograph being held in front of his face, but he could not smell the burning smoke from the pots. Behind the fog of smoke he saw the priest's eyes silently, and suddenly his nose could smell the smoke but he was smelling gunpowder. He blinked and was back in the slaughterhouse. Looking behind him he saw the faces of the people in line and they looked like drunk people at a party suddenly beginning to sober up, their faces now taking in every detail and sound and smell around them. The faces looked ready to shout, to panic, to fight.

At that moment when anything could happen, Lupov heard the voice of the small man who should have been a street conductor begin talking, his indifferent voice hypnotic, then like a drug, just like the priests Lupov had hated as a boy but always obeyed. "Comrades!" he said loudly. "Comrades, comrades, let me tell you a story."

Like children waiting for a bedtime story the terrified people in line behind Lupov waited silently.

"Before the revolution," the small man said, talking to the floor, "when I was a boy I worked in a slaughter-house for pigs. Oh the noise those pigs would make. In my bed at night I would still hear those pigs! I couldn't eat sausages or ham for years!" He smiled and was shaking his head at the memory. "I would still be there today, but our great socialist revolution has freed us workers to have better jobs than our fathers, and our children will have better jobs than us..."

The small man stopped talking as the eight men with pistols finished re-loading their pistols. He scratched his ear and turned towards the sobbing boy standing in front of Lupov. The small man's eyes never looked at the boy's eyes or face, but he said tenderly in a low voice, "Comrade, hush! Be brave! Do you want to upset the women?"

The sound of the boy sobbing stopped.

"That's it," said the small man to the boy. "Now come along, we don't have all day. I haven't had my supper yet."

The small man ushered the boy and Lupov forward towards the doors, and the index finger of his right hand was counting six more people behind them.

Lupov walked behind the naked boy to the doors and the boy faced the first door and Lupov looked at the boy's face wet from crying, the eyes full of terror like an animal caught in a hunter's steel trap. Lupov's head turned to his right, staring at the two pretty young women with ivory white bodies and long brown hair, and both were holding hands and their eyes were locked and saying goodbye. What could they have done to end up here?

I must be dreaming, he told himself. It is all a bad dream. You are having a dream you fool, it is only a dream, only a dream...He closed his eyes and the stink of gunpowder was in his nostrils and he wondered how he could smell something in a dream? Lupov's eyes snapped open and he turned around, frowning at the smoke and behind it the gunmen.

It wasn't a dream.

This was really happening.

"Face the door!" screamed the man in charge of the firing squad.

Lupov immediately turned and faced the door, wanting to scream, his chest rising and falling as he breathed faster and faster. He looked at all the bullet holes in the door, counting them, his fingers afraid to touch the holes, and his huge body was shaking with anger. He saw his fists pounding like hammers on the door and he heard himself shouting at the door full of bullet-holes, "I am Lupov! I am Lupov!"

Behind him a voice screamed "Fire!"

The End

CHAPTER 10

Voodoo Doll

Today was Charlie Pigowitz's Birthday and he was 58 years old, but he knew only his Mother would remember his Birthday.

Charlie's short round body was wedged tightly into the back of the Taxi bringing him home from the college where he taught a film class six hours a day five days a week to his apartment building. On his knees was the soft brown leather case with a handle that had been with him since his first day teaching the film class 21 years ago, and it was full of his student's test papers.

His apartment was less than half-a-mile from his college so the Taxi ride was very short, and when the Taxi stopped at his apartment building he always waited for the driver to get out and open his door like a chauffer opening the door of a Limo, because if famous people in the film industry had their car doors opened for them then why shouldn't someone who should have been famous like him get the same treatment?

The Taxi driver was thin and tall and stood stiffly as he opened Charlie's door, and after Charlie struggled to free himself from the back of the car and was standing next to the driver, the driver's tall thin body and thick hair and pleasant face made Barny look even shorter and fatter and balder and uglier.

The Taxi Driver said, "Have a good day Mr. Pigowitz. I'll see you tomorrow morning." Charlie Pigowitz ignored the driver and waddled like a fat penguin towards the main entrance of his six-story sandstone coloured brick apartment building.

Standing at the double glass doors at the entrance of his building, the doors were like a mirror and he could see his disappointing reflection. His big round body hadn't lost or gained more than a few pounds since he was in his 20's, and his big round smooth face was the face of a man in his 30s, not a man pushing 60. His small dark cruel eyes looked like the dead eyes of a shark, and the short curly black hair on his almost bald head looked like it was dyed with black ink, but it was his natural hair colour.

Charlie's small chubby hand was holding a key and as always he had trouble getting the key in the lock, his awkward fingers poking the key at the lock again and again until it finally fit. He pushed open one of the double glass doors, and waddled along the dark blue carpet straight down the main hallway to the first door on the right, and a second key in his chubby small hand began poking the key at the lock until it finally fit. He pushed open his apartment door and stepped inside, and as he closed the door behind him he was out of breath and gasping for air.

His big soft leather chair in the middle of his living room looked so far away, and he took a deep breath and began waddling towards the chair. He fell backwards into the chair and felt its smooth soft welcoming embrace, his soft body and the chair melting together and becoming one.

Charlie's chair was facing a huge TV screen, and to the right of the TV was the tripod film screen with its screen pulled up. On his left beside his chair was a small table with a pile of DVDs and an old-fashioned film projector without a film reel on it, and on his right beside his chair an identical small table with his snacks and bottles of soda pop. His small dark eyes were full of lust as they leered at the snack table's candy bars and bags of chips and pop bottles. His right hand quickly grabbed one of the candy bars and both hands tore away the wrapper and he shoved the entire bar into his mouth and began chewing and sucking the mouth full of chocolate like he hadn't eaten for days.

Charlie's eyes looked at the small table on his left, which had piles of DVDs. He didn't want to walk all that way to the TV screen to put a DVD in the DVD player. He heard his cell phone ringing and his eyes followed the ringing to the table on his left that was covered with snacks and bottles of pop, and he saw the cell phone he couldn't find that day at work. He picked up the phone and announced, "Pigowitz here." He listened a few seconds and said, "Hello, Mother. You remembered my

Birthday!"

Charlie pressed the phone hard against his ear, trying to hear his Mother's soft weak voice. "Thank you Mother. I know how much you miss Father, but you did get to say goodbye to him. Now Mother don't cry. What? Yes, I'm well. I don't sound well? I'm just tired. I haven't been sleeping well. Oh, just bad dreams. I have this dream where I'm back in school and some boys are chasing me, and they yell Piggy! Piggy! Piggy! But before they catch me I always wake up."

Charlie Pigowitz was smirking as he said "It wasn't your faut Mother." Charlie's greedy little eyes were locked on the table full of snacks beside him as he listened to his phone, and finally he said, "Well thank you for calling Mother. You're the only one who wished me a Happy Birthday. Now I have a lot of school papers to mark, so goodnight." He listened to his Mother saying goodbye, and pressed the icon on the phone that hung up. Mother is going to start crying now, thought Charlie, and it made him feel good.

Charlie grabbed a big full soda bottle on the table, took off the cap, and drank half of the bottle without stopping. Putting the bottle back on the table he grabbed at the candy bars and peeled away the wrappers, stuffing the brown bars into his mouth until his cheeks were bulging like a cartoon squirl. His happy round face was at war with the mouth full of chocolate and it was winning, his throat gulping down the chocolate without choking then his hand grabbed the half empty soda bottle and drank it empty without stopping.

Some chocolate was smeared on his face, and when he saw the melted chocolate on his fingertips and wiped them on his shirt where it covered his male breasts. Charlie wondered if he should have told his Mother about his dreams, but she and his dead Father really were to blame for the way the Bullies had tortured him and gotten away with it. As the memories returned, his face darkened and was full of hate and pain, and he began echoing the boys chasing him, his voice rising as he shouted "Here Piggy! Piggy! Piggy! We're gonna catch you Piggy! Come back here Piggy!"

Charlie Pigowitz was breathing hard, his chest rising and falling as his hand gripped the chair's armrests. He looked to his left at the table with stacks of DVD's and an old-fashioned film projector. He didn't want to walk all the way to the TV with a DVD, so picked up his remote control and pointed it at the TV screen and watched the big empty screen burst to life with colour and sound. He pointed the remote at a subscription channel he paid for that showed Foreign Films with English sub-titles and dubbed English voices. He pointed the remote at the film index and selected a film he had watched dozens of times called "Heads Will Roll" about an ancient Chinese warlord. The film popped on the screen and he pointed the remote at the word PLAY and pressed the remote's OK button.

The film came to life on the screen, the Chinese music wailing loudly as it tried to set the mood for ancient China. And there he was on the screen, the great warlord in all his armour and glory, sitting on his horse. A peasant messenger ran to the emperor and threw himself on the ground. "Great Emperor, the city beyond those hills has revolted! They have proclaimed a new emperor!"

The Warlord's round savage face twisted in the direction of the city, his eyes burning with a desire for revenge. "Heads will roll!" he shouted, and behind him his warriors in their shiny helmets and shiny heavy armor cheered. He looked at the messenger squirming on the ground and said "How dare you bring me such bad news on the day my daughter is to be married!" The messenger was shaking with fear as the warlord looked at the warrior closest to him and his hand made a short quick gesture towards the messenger that made the warrior jump off his horse, draw his sword, and swing his sword down hard on the neck of the messenger.

Charlie Pigowitz laughed, and when he laughed he always made a barking sound. His cruel dark eyes were staring at the warlord with the same love Charlie had every time he looked in a mirror. He was wishing he was sitting on the horse wearing that armour, and as the warlord turned to shout his order again Charlie shouted the words with him, their voices blending together: "Heads will roll!" Charlie was suddenly very tired, and closed his eyes. He opened his eyes and the movie was over.

Charlie reached down for his leather case and pulled it up onto his lap, reaching in and pulling out 60 papers. They were all one-page movie reviews of the student's favorite films. He told the students to see if they could do a review in only one page because that would show what good writers they were or weren't, but the real reason was he didn't want to read more than 60 pages. He took the 10 pages on the top of the pile, and pulled a red marker out of the chest pocket of his shirt, and as he glanced at each paper he wrote the grade B at the top of the page. He put the 10 papers back in his case, and quickly began writing the grade C- at the top of the other 50 papers without even glancing at those papers.

The moment he finished and was sliding the 50 papers into his case, his cell phone began ringing. His right hand scooped up the phone and pressed it to his ear. "Pigowitz here!" he declared, his voice booming like the Chinese warlord he had just watched. "Oh, Hello Vice President Summers! What can I do for you?" asked Charlie, grinning from ear-to-ear. He listened for a full minute, then said, "Of course parents are complaining. How can I make over 100 students famous film Directors." He listened for another full minute, and said, "Yes, I told my class to go for lunch then gave a test to the ones who stayed in the class. Did you ask them what I said? I told them you don't have to go if you don't want to. And they went anyway, so they weren't there to take the test."

Charlie heard the voice in the phone shouting and cursing, and waited for a chance to speak. "Well if these kids can't survive my class, how will they ever survive if they do get hired by the film industry? If they think I'm jerking them around and playing mind games, wait until a Producer or Director starts screaming at them.

What? No, I'm not screaming at students." Charlie looked at the stack of test papers as he listened to the voice in the phone, and replied, "No, I don't just mark 10 papers and give all the other students bad grades. In fact I just finished marking papers when you phoned."

Charlie listened as the voice in the phone complained for several minutes, and when the voice stopped talking Charlie said, "Even If I did mark only 10 papers, so what? How can I be a mentor to more than 10 students? You don't even have enough film equipment for 10 people!" Charlie listened for another minute, and said, "If the parents want refunds, that's not my department. Why don't you talk to my Union. Last time you phoned me at home they made you apologize. Good night, vice president."

Charlie Pigowitz hung up the cell phone, put it on the table, and felt like he was on top of the world. He pointed his remote control at the TV screen so he could play the film about the warlord again. Before he could press the OK button, his apartment's buzzer rang next to the door. Charlie frowned, and the arm pointing at the TV screen lowered. The buzzer buzzed again, and the curiosity was unbearable. Charlie put down the remote, waddled to the door, and pressed the intercom button. "Pigowitz here," he said into the intercom.

There was no answer.

He turned and started moving towards the chair but was stopped by the buzzer ringing again. He turned and walked back, opened the door, and waddled to the main entrance. Maybe my intercom is broken, he thought. He pressed his face against one of the double glass doors, his small eyes staring into the night, then stepped back and was turning when it caught his eyes. A round paper package was outside the doors leaning against the building.

Charlie smiled and his heart beat faster. Had somebody besides his mother remembered his Birthday? Charlie quickly opened one of the glass doors and stepped outside, and as he bent to pick up the round parcel he heard the loud ripping sound of the seat of his pants ripping open. He stood up and looked around, making sure nobody had seen or heard that. He examined the parcel and written on the paper was "For Mr. Charlie Pigowitz." "Somebody remembered my Birthday! said Charlie as he studied the parcel and waddled back inside.

He was full of energy as he reached his open apartment door. Inside his apartment he tore away the brown paper, and gazed lovingly at the reel of old film that would fit on his film projector. He looked at his film projector like a child looking at a magical toy. His awkward short fingers became nimble and expertly attached the film reel to the back of his projector, threaded the film through the spools and back up to the empty film reel at the front of the projector that would pull the film up past the light of the projector at 32 frames a second to shine the film frames on a screen as the film strip wound onto the empty reel. To the left of his TV was the film screen sitting on a metal tripod.

He pointed the projector at the film screen that looked like a small white sail of a toy boat. His thumb pushed the tiny switch that turned on the projector and the magic toy was spinning it's reels and flashing the film onto the screen.

Charlie Pigowitz sat down in his chair and stared at the screen, and the image that came on the screen made the screen look like a mirror. On the screen was a man who looked like Charlie's identical twin, and he was dressed like Charlie and sitting in a chair that looked like Charlie's chair. Charlie and the Charlie on the screen stared at each other, the sound of the film projector hypnotic. Minutes passed and Charlie couldn't move, the image on the screen filling his brain and controlling his brain. He had always loved movies, living and breathing movies, always living in the characters on the screen and laughing when they laughed and crying when they cried until he became that character, but this was different. That was him on the screen, him and nobody else, and he didn't have to be someone else to live on that scree. He was living on that screen as himself, as the most beautiful image ever on a film screen, and Charlie felt himself leave his body and float towards the screen and enter the body of the man on the screen. Suddenly he was back in his chair and he saw his double's right hand claw at his chest and a look of terrific pain on his double's face and a moment later it felt like a big fist punched him in the chest and his right hand was clawing at his chest just like his double on the screen. The man on the screen's mouth fell open and he slumped forward and Charlie's mouth fell open and he slumped forward and another big invisible fist smashed into his chest and his mouth opened to scream but no sound came out. Charlie fell back into his chair, his head hanging down and his small lifeless eyes staring at the floor. Moments later the film reel ran out of film and the last strip of film that left the now empty reel was on the now full reel, flapping loose as the reel spun round and round, it hypnotic noise the only sound in the room.

The End.

CHAPTER 11

The Crucified Mailman

"Do you think it really happened, Mack?"

"Don't talk so loud, Jones, there may be German snipers," said the biggest man in the group of four soldiers. All four wore army caps that looked like police caps and khaki colored Canadian army uniforms, and they carried their rifles slung over their shoulders as they walked south into the dark night towards the burning ruins of the Belgian city of Ypres.

Private Jones lowered his voice, and said, "Mack, I have to know. Did the Germans crucify one of our sergeants to a Belgian Barn with bayonets?"

"How many times you gonna ask me that?" asked Private McKinley, who the other three had nicknamed "Mack." McKinley was a big, powerfully built man who had worked as a lumberjack in Canada and the U.S., and he was the group's natural leader who had earned their respect with his cool nerves, fairness, and common-sense.

"Stop talking about it Jones," said Private Nichols.

"Smith, what do you think?" asked Jones.

"I was thinking these farms in Belgium are making me homesick for my parent's farm in Canada," said Private Smith, trying to be a diplomat and change the subject. Smith was the quiet one in the group, but when he did speak everybody respected his opinion so much they often let him have the last word.

"In Canada we don't crucify people to Barn doors," said Jones stubbornly, refusing to let the subject dop.

"Everybody's talking about it, but nobody saw the body," said Smith.

Private Jones stopped walking, and said to his three friends. "We could be walkin' right into the German lines, and I want to know if it's true they crucify their prisoners. If I'm going to be stuck to a barn door with bayonets like that poor Bastard was two days ago, I'm not going to surrender."

"It's just a rumour," said Private Smith.

"Yeah Jones, stop believing every rumor you hear," said Private Nichols. "When we got to England all you talked about was how the Germans were cuttin' off the hands of Belgian babies. We've been in Belgium for weeks, and have you seen one baby with its hands cut off?"

"All the newspapers say its true," muttered Jones defensively.

"And you still believe Belgian farmers behind our lines

are signalling the Germans, telling them where to fire their cannons at us," said Nichols.

A moment later a cannon shell exploded to their right, shaking the ground under their boots like an earthquake, and all four men threw themselves on the ground. In the dark they looked like four short logs as they lay silent and motionless, and slowly all four heads lifted and looked to their right. The ground under them shook again and an exploding cannon shell's flash lit the outline of a tiny Belgian village.

All four soldiers lay on the ground several minutes, waiting for a third explosion, but the silence had returned. Mack was the first one to slowly stand up, and he was bent over ready to throw himself on the ground again. The other three slowly got up, and all four kept staring to their right where the two shells had fallen until they had walked a few hundred feet and the village was behind them.

Mack stopped walking and the other three stopped. Mack whispered, "That village is still holding out, so the Germans haven't broken through and surrounded us. If that village is St. Julian, we aren't far from the GHQ Line. Keep an eye out for our barbed wire."

Mack started walking and the other three followed him. The only sound they heard was their four pairs of boots stepping on the flat farmland. The four soldiers walked on silently, and they saw they were walking towards the dark shape of a fence and shed. All four men stopped at the fence, and Mack said, "Let's rest here a while."

"I'll take a look in the shed," said Jones, walking towards the shed as Mack leaned on the fence. Mack stared into the darkness in the direction they were heading, and said, "Shit, I'm really dying for a cigarette."

"Me too," said Smith.

"You light a cigarette, and we'll all be dead before you finish it," said Private Nichols. Nichols sat down with his back against the fence, and Smith sat down next to him.

"I know, I know," sighed Mack, his voice tired and his face miserable as he thought how long it could be before he could have his next cigarette. He looked over his shoulder at the glow on the northern horizon behind them that showed where the worst fighting was happening. "It looks like our guys are still holding back the Germans."

"I wish we could have brought more of them with us," said Private Nichols.

"Yeah, well, we all do," said Mack softly, the night not dark enough to hide the guilt on his face.

Jones walked back from the shed, and announced, "The shed is empty."

All four faces turned to stare north at the throbbing glow on the horizon from the flash of German cannon shells and the German star shells bursting in the air to cast green light on the battlefield and rob the defenders of the darkness. All four soldiers were imagining the horror of what their friends back there must be going through.

Private Nichols had to look away, his eyes staring down at his boots. He couldn't look at his three friends and kept staring down at his boots as he said, "I left a kid back there. He couldn't walk because of the poison gas. I was watching him suffocating. Only thing I could do for him was help him drink Rum from my canteen. He told me he was only 16, and he'd lied and said he was 19 so he could enlist. He was sitting on the ground trying to breathe and crying when I left, calling for his mother."

"Well he isn't suffering anymore," said Private Jones, his right hand making the sign of the cross on his chest like a good Catholic.

Private Nichols eyes lifted his eyes from his boots and returned to the horizon, and nobody made a sound as they stared at the red Hellish glow that looked like the bowels of Hell itself had opened.

Mac said in a loud voice full of authority, "Remember lads, when we get back, if they ask us why we didn't stay behind, we tell 'em our sergeant ordered us to fall back until we reached the GHQ Line. We all saw the Sergeant die from the poison gas, so they can't prove it's a lie." He thought a moment, and quickly added, "And don't say we were ordered to retreat, officers hate that word retreat. A sergeant would order us to retire, not retreat. Got it?"

Private's Jones and Smith grunted agreement.

"Jones, are you listening?"

"What's the difference between retreat and retire?" asked Jones.

Mack looked annoyed, but it was a fair question and he explained patiently, "If we retreat, it means we were defeated and forced off the battlefield by the enemy. But if we retire, it means we chose to pull back and weren't defeated."

"OK, Mack," said Jones, staring at the glowing horizon.

Mack sighed, his tired face angry as he spoke louder, "Jones, if they don't believe us, we could get put in front of a firing squad for desertion."

"Sure Mack, sure," said Jones, pulling his gaze from the horizon to Mack's angry face. "I know when to shut up."

For a moment Mack didn't know if he should kick Jones or laugh, but he laughed like a man who needed to laugh, and as he laughed everyone relaxed and Nichols chuckled and Smith smiled. They all knew they could trust each other with their lives, and that faith in each other had gotten them this far and could get them safely home.

"Mack, you really think they would shoot us?" asked Nichols. "No Canadians have ever faced a firing squad, only Brits."

"We are Brits," said Smith, looking confused.

"Our Canadian Division may be part of the British

Army, but Canadian officers are different," said Nichols wearily, sighing loudly and staring south.

"I'd rather be shot than crucified," said Jones, who was the only one now staring at the glowing horizon.

Mack shouted at Jones, "For Fuck's sake, will you shut up about being crucified!"

Jones eyes moved to Mack and he quickly interrupted him: "I wasn't talkin' about the Germans, Mack. I meant Field Punishment #2."

Jones saw all three of his friends staring at him, his mention of Field Punishment #2 grabbing their attention and filling them with worry. "A friend of mine has a pal who got Field Punishment #2.," said Jones. "They don't call it "Crucifixion" as a joke. He was taken inside a barn, spread-eagled on a wagon wheel, and had his hands hand-cuffed to the spokes. He was left like that 12 hours a day, for 12 days in a row."

"Why did they crucify him?" asked Smith.

"Falling asleep on guard duty," said Jones.

Nichols said, "I met a guy who was crucified, but he was tied to a fence. The ropes under his shoulders were pulled so tight, his arm sockets were almost pulled out of his body. He had to stand at that fence 12 hours a day for two weeks when it was raining and when the sun was so hot you could fry an egg in a pan without a fire."

Mack was nodding, pleased everybody fully understood how serious things could get if they didn't stick to their story. "We better get movin', the Germans could be plannin' another gas attack." Suddenly Mack lifted his right arm, signaling them to stop. Mack said, "Someone's out there."

Slowly all four men reached for the rifles hanging on their backs, grabbing their rifles shoulder straps to slide the rifles off their shoulders. Holding their rifles so they were pointing at the ground, they all stood stiff and silent as statues, their ears strained for the tiniest sound. All four men heard the sound of one pair of boots walking towards them.

The sound of the boots was growing louder, and out of the darkness stepped a soldier wearing a Canadian Army uniform and cap. On the arms of his khaki jacket were sergeant stripes. He was carrying what looked like a mailbag over his shoulder. Instantly all four rifles lifted and aimed at the stranger, who froze and stared with bulging eyes and a terrified face. Suddenly his fear vanished and his face was angry as he barked, "Lower those rifles at once, I'm a Canadian Sergeant."

All four soldiers stared at the large sergeant's stripes on the arms of the stranger's khaki jacket. Very slowly all four rifles lowered and were pointing at the ground, and Mack stepped forward and said, "Sorry Sir, we thought you might be a German."

"Good God Man, do I look like a German?" barked the furious Sergeant, ignoring the fact the soldiers had been right to be on guard. "Are there only four of you, or are there more?"

"Only the four of us, Sir," said Mack.

"Where's your sergeant?" demanded the Canadian Sergeant.

"Dead, Sir," said Mack.

The sergeant scowled. "Why aren't you with the rest of your Brigade?"

Mack was icy calm and said matter-of-factly, "When our sergeant was dying from the poison gas, he ordered us to retire to the GHQ Line to make a last stand against a German break-through."

The sergeant's lips had a cruel little smile, and he said in a low voice full of authority, "Is that so?" His cold eyes studied the faces of the other three soldiers. His eyes fixed on Jones, and like a strict schoolmaster confronting a schoolboy he asked, "Do you have anything to add to that, Private?"

"No sir!" said Jones.

The Sergeant shifted his attention to Private Smith. "Private, why would your sergeant order you to fall back?"

Smith spoke fast and had never sounded more convincing as he explained, "Our rifles were jamming, and we have no way to protect ourselves from another poison gas attack."

The Sergeant's eyes studied Private Smith, trying to decide if he was a coward or a good soldier helpless without a Sergeant telling him what to do. "Private, do you want the Germans pushing the British Army into the sea? If they break through here, they'll capture Ypres, then its only 20 miles to the English Channel. Do you understand?"

Nichols frowned. "Yes, Sir. But how can we stop another poison gas attack?"

"The same way we stopped the first gas attack," explained the Sergeant. "You get a handkerchief, pee on it, and press it against your face. Your urine stops the chlorine in the gas from getting in your lungs."

"Sergeant, how close are we to the GHQ Line?" asked Smith.

"Private," he said slowly, "Nobody is defending the GHQ Line. Its an empty trench. Every Battalion is at half-strength, and every man who can fire a rifle is two miles north,"—The Sergeant's right hand pointed north, where the four soldiers had come from—"And one mile west," and his hand was pointing to the right of the path the four soldiers were walking. As he pointed to his right, his finger moved back a little to the place where the two cannon shells had exploded. "You just walked past St. Julien Village. It's being held by less than 200 Canadians. If the Germans capture it, the Canadian Division could be surrounded."

Mack said to the sergeant, "Excuse me sir, but why are you out here all alone?"

The sergeant scowled. "Well, private, as you can see I'm carrying a mailbag. My Brigade HQ sent me to deliver letters and parcels to our men in the front line trenches."

"Your delivering mail?" blurted out Jones, amazed that Sergeants were acting as mailmen on a battlefield while the soldiers were being blown out of their Trenches by cannon shells.

"I'm following orders!" barked the Sergeant.

Smith said quickly, "Nobody told us mail was being delivered to the front lines."

Mack said, "Sir, can you tell us how far it is to the GHQ Line?"

"Your not going to the GHQ Line," said the sergeant. "Your sergeant is dead, and I'm giving the orders now. We need every man in the Canadian Division in the front line trenches stopping the German attack. So turn around and go back, that's an order."

"Yes Sir!" said all four privates with one voice.

"I'd take you back myself," said the Sergeant, "But I have to deliver mail to St. Julien. They have letters to send home, and the letters they get might be the last ones they'll ever read." The sergeant began walking towards the village where they had seen the two explosions, and the four soldiers began slowly walking north. They walked for a full minute, then Mack stopped walking. He turned around, and as he walked back towards the fence the other three soldiers followed him.

As they reached the fence, they saw the dark shape of the Sergeant waiting for them. "Where are you men going?" barked the Sergeant, stepping forward out of the darkness.

"Our Sergeant ordered us back to the GHQ Line," said Mack.

"What's your name, Private?" barked the Sergeant.

"Private Philip McKinley," said Mack.

"Private McKinley," announced the Sergeant, "For refusing to obey orders and deserting in the face of the enemy, I am sentencing you to Field Punishment #2. Your punishment will begin immediately." The Sergeant's hot eyes stared at the other three soldiers. He said loudly, "Men, take his rifle."

The other three soldiers all turned their heads to look at Mack and wait for his orders.

The Sergeant's face was swollen red with rage, and he screamed, "I'm the one giving the orders!"

None of the three soldiers moved. The terrible silence was broken by Smith, who said, "Sir, we don't have any rope."

"Well find some!" barked the Sergeant. "Look in the shed."

"It's empty," said Jones.

"Well look again!" barked the Sergeant. As Jones turned towards the shed, the Sergeant's eyes fixed on the rifle strap hanging from Jones' rifle. "Wait! We don't need rope, we'll use your rifle slings," commanded the Sergeant.

Jones watched the Sergeant walk towards him, and as the Sergeant examined the rifle sling his square face scowled. The Sergeant's eyes lifted from the rifle sling to Jones' face. He said in a low, menacing voce, "Private, that's a German Mauser. Where's your Canadian Rifle?"

"I threw it away, Sir."

"Why?"

"It's a piece of shit, Sir."

"Throwing away your rifle is a court martial offense," said the Sergeant.

"Sir, have you fired that rifle?" asked Jones. "Our rifle bolts kept jamming if we fired too fast, or if they got a bit of dust in them. Half the men were throwing away their rifles and grabbing German or British rifles they found on the ground."

The Sergeant stared at Private Smith's rifle. "Another German Mauser." The Sergeant's eyes kept staring at Smith's German rifle as he called out, "Private McKinley, do you have your Ross Rifle?"

"I have a British Lee Enfield, Sergeant," said Mack.

"I've got mine, Sir," said Nichols. Stepping forward, he lifted the rifle to his waist, and tried pulling back the bolt but it was stuck.

"The Ross Rifle is the world's finest target Rifle," declared the Sergeant like a door-to-door salesman trying to sell the rifle to a customer. "It doesn't matter if a few jam from not being cleaned properly, because we will never stop the Germans with bullets or cannon shells.

The only thing the German fears is the bayonet, and you have to push him back with a bayonet charge. As soon as he sees cold steel, he'll run. Then we unleash the Cavalry to finish him off." The Sergeant reached into his jacket's chest pocket, plucked out a little notebook and pen, and flipping the notebook open he ordered, "Right! I want all your names!"

The Sergeant waited, and when nobody answered he looked up and saw all three faces in front of him were staring past his shoulder. As he turned to see what they were staring at he saw Mack standing close behind him and swinging his rifle like a baseball bat towards his head. The Sergeant's right arm lifted to protect his head as the rifle crashed into his arm and face, knocking him backwards and sending his army cap and notebook and pen flying through the air. The Sergeant fell back against the fence and his head cracked loudly against a fence post.

His body lay on the ground, his arms and legs twitching and his eyes staring crazily upwards at nothing. Mack bent down, put his hands under the sergeant's armpits, and looked at the soldier standing closest to him, Jones. Jones rushed forward and helped Mack lift the body. As Mack tipped the standing body back against the fence, he reached for the handle of the bayonet he wore on his belt. His left hand was on the Sergeant's throat as his right hand holding the bayonet jerked back then thrust forward so deep into the Sergeant's groin the bayonet's tip stuck in the fence.

Jones slid his bayonet out of it's scabbard. Pushing the steel tip into the sergeant's left shoulder, he kept pushing until the bayonet touched the wood, then he used the palm of his hand to pound the bayonet deeper into the wood.

Nichols and Smith were each holding their long bayonets as they walked towards the Sergeant. Nichol's thrust his bayonet into the Sergeant's right shoulder hard enough for the bayonet to stick in the fence. Mack let go of the body and moved away as Smith crouched down and thrust his bayonet deep into the sergeant's right leg.

As Smith stepped back, Mack moved closer to the body, his left hand reaching for the sergeant's hair to lift his head so he could see if the eyes were alive or dead. Mack spat in the dead man's face, then he let go of the hair and the head fell forward.

Mack picked up his Lee Enfield, and saw the Sergeant's blood on its wooden stock. Lifting the rifle above his head like an axe, and swung it down so hard at the top fence post next to the Sergeant's head the rifle stock broke and fell on the ground. Mack tossed the rifle's barrel onto the ground next to the stock. He looked behind him at his three comrades and said, "Lets get rid of anything that could identify him."

Mack bent down and reached inside the almost empty

mailbag, pulling out a few dozen letters and tearing them up. He was dropping the torn paper in a pile, and as he walked around picking up letters that had fallen on the ground the other three soldiers were removing every kind of ID from the body. As Mack tore up the last letters and tossed them into the pile, Jones handed him the sergeant's small paybook that had his name, rank, and description so he could be identified by the paymaster as he was paid his army salary. Mack asked Jones, "Did anybody read this?"

"No," said Jones.

"Good," said Mack. "We don't need to know who he was." At that Mack tore the paybook into small pieces, and tossed them on the ground.

"We have everything," announced Smith, his cupped hands full of Brass uniform buttons with the man's Battalion number, the two round discs on the cord he had worn around his neck, a ring with an inscription inside, and a wristwatch with an inscription on the back." Mack picked up the mailbag, holding it open so Smith could pour all the items into the bag. As Smith poured the items from his hands into the bag Mack said, "We'll carry this stuff with us, then stop and bury it."

Smith asked Mack, "Are you sure he's dead?"

"Fuck him," growled Mack.

The four soldiers walked away, none of them looking back as the sun began rising on their right.

That evening at sunset, a small group of Canadian soldiers were walking south towards the fence and shed.
Five men, all of them privates, saw the grey shapes of
the fence and shed 200 yards away. One of the men,
Private Barrie, said "Two of us better check it out." He
looked at Private White, and the man stepped forward.
They walked side-by-side towards the fence. Barrie put
out his arm to stop the other man. He pointed at the
shape the looked like a man leaning against the fence.
Barrie cupped his hand to his mouth and shouted,
"Hello!"

The dark shape didn't move.

Private Barrie said, "Follow me. And watch for snipers."
The two soldiers moved carefully towards the fence,
crouching down as they walked in case it was a trap
and they had to take cover. As soon as they were close
enough to see the man was pinned to the fence with
four bayonets, his head hanging forward, they stopped
and stared.

"I hope that poor bastard is dead," said Private Barrie.
They stopped crouching and walked towards the body
and stopped when the were close enough to reach out
and touch him. The soldier crouched down and looked
into the man's deathly white face at the open eyes.
Looking over his shoulder at White, he saw White was
holding his rifle and his hand pulled back on the rifle
bolt and pushed it forward, making a loud CLICK-CLICK

sound as a bullet slid into the rifle barrel.

Barrie said to White, "He's dead."

"He must be that Canadian sergeant crucified to a barn everybody's been talking about for the last two days," said White, staring at the sergeant stripes on the dead man's khaki jacket.

"I don't see the ruins of a Barn," said Barrie, looking around the empty field for some trace of a Barn. "But this must be the sergeant."

"What do you think happened?" asked White.

Barrie said, "He probably led a few men out on patrol, and they ran into some Germans. He got caught, the others got away." He pointed at the Sergeant's uniform. "Look, they took all his buttons, so we don't know what Battalion he belonged to." Barry pulled at the neck of the dead man's shirt, and said, "They took his ID discs too. The Germans like souvenirs as much as we do."

"He put up a good fight, sir," said the other soldier, pointing at two pieces of a broken British Rifle on the ground. Private Barrie looked down at the broken rifle with dried blood on the stock, and the small pile of torn letters. A light breeze suddenly carried away a few pieces of paper, and the corporal bent down and picked up a handful of torn papers.

"Why didn't the Germans take his letters?" asked the other soldier. "We give all the German letters we find to the lads in the intelligence branch."

"He must have been popular, getting so many letters. His name and address will be on all the letters," said Barrie. He picked up pieces of torn letters, and said, "This piece has his first name...Sergeant..." As he tried reading the writing, he said "And this piece has his last name...and his address in Canada."

"We can't leave him like this, can we?" asked White.

"No," said Barrie. Both men struggled with the body, pulling out the bayonets and slowly, carefully lowering the body onto the ground. Barry looked at the four Bayonets on the ground, and said, "Only one bayonet is Canadian. Two are German, and one is British. The Germans must be running out of rifles and ammunition." He looked back at where the other three soldiers were standing, then up at the grey sky. "It will be light out soon, and the German snipers will be able to see us."

The two men began walking quickly away from the fence towards their three fellow soldiers 20 yards away. Barry saw the other soldier looking over his shoulder, and said gently, "Don't look back, you'll give yourself nightmares."

"The Germans will never take me alive," said the Private White.

The End

Made in the USA
Monee, IL
22 May 2021